We'll Prescribe You a Cat

We'll Prescribe You a Cat

Syou Ishida

Translated from the Japanese by
E. Madison Shimoda

Berkley
New York

BERKLEY
An imprint of Penguin Random House LLC
penguinrandomhouse.com

First published in the United Kingdom, in 2024,
by Doubleday, an imprint of Transworld.
Transworld is part of the Penguin Random House group of companies.

Originally published in Japan as *Neko Wo Shoho Itashimasu*
by PHP Institute, Inc., in 2023.

Publication rights for this English edition arranged through
The Appleseed Agency Ltd., Japan.

Library of Congress Cataloging-in-Publication Data

Names: Syou, Ishida, 1975- author. | Shimoda, E. Madison, translator.
Title: We'll prescribe you a cat / Syou Ishida;
translated from the Japanese by E. Madison Shimoda.
Other titles: Neko o shohō itashimasu. English | We will prescribe you a cat
Description: New York: Berkley, 2024.
Identifiers: LCCN 2024008204 (print) | LCCN 2024008205 (ebook) |
ISBN 9780593818749 (hardcover) | ISBN 9780593818756 (ebook)
Subjects: LCGFT: Novels.
Classification: LCC PL880.4.Y68 N4513 2024 (print) |
LCC PL880.4.Y68 (ebook) | DDC 895.63/6—dc23/eng/20240505
LC record available at https://lccn.loc.gov/2024008204
LC ebook record available at https://lccn.loc.gov/2024008205

Printed in the United States of America
5th Printing

Interior illustrations by Alissa Levy
Book design by Alison Cnockaert

Bee

1

Bee

Shuta Kagawa stood at the end of a shadowy alley, gazing up at a multipurpose building. After getting thoroughly lost, he had finally arrived. The structure looked like it had been built to fill the narrow gap between two apartment blocks.

"Is this it?" he mumbled.

He'd doubted there could be anywhere that his phone's navigation app couldn't find, but this place proved otherwise. From the alley, the sky looked distant and hazy, and there was no sunlight. The air felt humid; the building looked old and grimy.

"What's up with the address anyway?"

East of Takoyakushi Street, south of Tominokoji Street,

west of Rokkaku Street, north of Fuyacho Street, Nakagyō Ward, Kyoto.

This kind of address was unique to Kyoto. Instead of official street numbers, it gave the names of the streets that intersected in four directions. The instructions were so vague that most nonlocals found them confusing. Shuta had been meandering around the neighborhood for some time. Just when he was about to give up, he spotted the narrow opening to the alleyway.

Why do Kyoto residents bother with such cryptic directions?

To Shuta, who hailed from another prefecture, Kyoto's street names were like a code. Even something as simple as an address had an obliqueness that seemed designed to keep outsiders away.

He lingered for a moment in the dark alley, let out a deep sigh, then gathered himself, determined not to be disappointed just yet. Just because the building was in a sketchy location didn't necessarily mean the tenants were sketchy, too. Maybe the apartment buildings had been constructed around this building after it had been built, and you couldn't say there wasn't a kind of hideaway feel to the place.

The entrance to the building was open, no elevator, just a staircase at the back. It was dimly lit, or maybe it just felt that way because there were so few people around. He walked down the hallway, eyeing the signs on the doors. It seemed like some sort of commercial building full of shady businesses.

Soon, I might be making scam phone calls to elderly people from an office in a building like this, he thought, glimpsing his own future. He shook his head. He'd come here to make sure that didn't happen.

He climbed the stairs to his destination, Nakagyō Kokoro Clinic for the Soul, situated on the fifth floor. An old, solid-looking door swung open with unnerving ease. He took a quick peek inside—the clinic was surprisingly well lit. There was a small reception window by the entrance, which appeared unattended.

"Hello?" Shuta called.

Silence. He wondered if he'd arrived during a break. He stood with his arms crossed. Not having the clinic's contact details, he hadn't been able to make an appointment.

"Hello?" he called out again, a little louder this time.

He heard the muted tapping of slippers against the floor, and a nurse appeared, a pale woman in her late twenties.

"How can I help you?" she asked.

"I don't have an appointment, but I was hoping I could see the doctor," Shuta said.

"You're a patient, I see. Please come in." The nurse spoke the Kansai dialect with a leisurely intonation unique to Kyoto. Her accent was quite pronounced for someone so young.

There was a sofa at the back of the waiting room, but the nurse led Shuta right past it and directly into the examination room. It was smaller even than his company's smoking room and modestly furnished with a desk, a computer, and two chairs.

Is this really the famous clinic? Shuta grew more anxious. Every psychiatrist's office he'd ever known had been spacious and well appointed. Not only were those clinics *not* located in old, uninviting buildings, but they saw patients by appointment only. Patients were also required to complete lengthy medical intake forms that took nearly an hour to fill out. He appreciated being able to see the doctor so easily here, but, come to think of it, he hadn't even given them his health insurance details.

The curtains in the back flew open, and a youngish, slight man in a white lab coat appeared.

"Hello, there. This must be your first time at our clinic." He spoke with quite a high, nasally voice in a comforting Kyoto cadence that didn't come across as overly familiar.

"How did you hear about us?"

"Um . . ." For a moment, Shuta was at a loss for an explanation. He considered lying but decided to be honest. "I heard about you indirectly. A former colleague told me about his younger brother's wife's cousin's company's client's client who sees you and recommended this clinic."

He had found himself here on the basis of some information that was less reliable than dregs from a rumor mill. All he'd been told was the clinic's name and that it was located on the fifth floor of a building with a cryptic address.

This wasn't his first time at a psychiatric clinic. He'd had several previous sessions six months ago. Even then, he didn't have high hopes of any improvement, but he felt he needed to make an effort to get better. He researched online for highly rated psychiatrists, seeing one after another until he'd been to every single psychiatrist near his home and office. That was how he'd ended up here. It was a last resort. He just hadn't expected the clinic to be in such a desolate spot.

"Well, we've got a little situation here. Truth is, I'm not accepting any new patients right now. I run a small practice—it's just the nurse and me."

Shuta frowned. *I guess this place is also a no-go. They call their practices "Clinic for the Soul" or whatever, but when it comes down to it, few doctors care enough to help you with your problems. Well, fine, then.*

He was about to say this out loud when the doctor

broke into a broad grin, and his eyes took on the gleam of a mischievous child's.

"I'll make an exception this time, since you're a referral."

The space, already so narrow that their knees almost touched, grew even more intimate. The doctor turned to his desk. Shuta watched as the doctor's fingers flew across the keyboard as he typed into his computer.

"Name and age?"

All of a sudden, the session had started.

"Shuta Kagawa. Twenty-five years old."

"So, what brings you here today?"

Shuta gave a little shiver. He'd seen this scenario play out before. Each doctor had given him the same answer.

That's tough. You don't have to work so hard.

It's good that you came to see me. Thank you.

Then they would all prescribe him similar medications. It wasn't the doctors but the sleeping pills that had helped.

"I . . ."

Insomnia, tinnitus, loss of appetite.

Whenever work crossed his mind, his chest constricted, his breathing turned shallow, and sleep eluded him. His symptoms were so common that the doctors never thought anything of them. This time, he was determined to explain his condition properly and overcome it once and for all. But before he knew it, his true feelings slipped out.

"I want to quit my job."

"Is that so?" the doctor replied.

Shuta realized what he'd said. "Oh, no. I didn't mean it like that. I don't *actually* want to quit. I want to figure out how to carry on working at my current company. I work for a major brokerage firm—you know, the kind that you see in commercials. The thing is, it's run like a sweatshop."

"I see," said the doctor. Then he broke into another smile. "We'll prescribe you a cat. Let's keep an eye on your condition." He spun around in his chair and called out to the back. "Chitose, can you bring the cat?"

"Sure," answered a voice from behind the curtains. The pale nurse from earlier entered. There was a luster in her eyes that Shuta hadn't noticed before. She was beautiful in an understated way. Shooting Shuta a wry look, she asked brusquely, "Are you sure he's right for this, Dr. Nikké?"

"Absolutely."

What an odd place, and Nikké—what a weird name.

The nurse placed a pet carrier on the desk and silently slipped away. Inside the plastic crate was a cat.

Shuta was at a loss for words. He stared unblinkingly at the cat before him.

It is an actual cat. Gray, unremarkable, ordinary.

The cat sat partially in shadow, but its large round eyes shimmered with a golden hue. It looked warily back at Shuta.

"So, Mr. Kagawa, let's try this for a week."

". . ."

"I'm writing you a prescription."

"You're writing me a prescription?"

"Correct."

Shuta looked at the cat in the carrier.

"Is that . . . a cat?"

"It is."

Shuta was starting to question his sanity.

"A real cat?"

"Of course. They're very effective. You know the old saying: 'A cat a day keeps the doctor away.' Cats are more effective than any other medicine out there."

That doesn't make any sense.

The doctor handed Shuta a small piece of paper. "Here's your prescription form. Please take it to reception, and you'll be given what you need. I'll see you again in a week. Now, I have another patient waiting . . ." He indicated the door as if to say *You can go now.*

Shuta snapped out of his daze. He felt laughter welling within him.

"I see what this is," he said with a chuckle. "This is what they call animal-assisted therapy, right?"

The doctor didn't respond but sat back in his chair with an inscrutable look.

"Is it part of your therapy to take your patients by surprise? Now I see why you haven't posted any details about the clinic anywhere. I sure panicked for a moment there. Prescribing cats . . . That's pretty interesting."

He placed his nose close to the carrier and peered inside. The cat widened its eyes and returned his gaze. Shuta knew nothing about animals, but this cat seemed equally bewildered.

"The cat's very cute, but it doesn't seem to like me much."

"Hmm? Let me see."

The doctor leaned in so close that their cheeks almost touched. Shuta was startled, but the doctor seemed unconcerned. The tip of the doctor's nose grazed the carrier's mesh panel as he stared at the cat within.

"Hmm? What do you think, cat?" He placed his ear to the mesh panel. "Yes, yes. She says it's all good."

"She said no such thing. She looks scared to me."

"Scared? Let me see." The doctor placed his nose even closer to the carrier, so close that it made Shuta nervous.

"What do you think, cat? You're good, right?" He looked up at Shuta and smiled. "She says she's good."

"The thing is, cats don't feel comfortable around people like me, who aren't used to them. Even if it's for the sake of therapy, it seems unfair to the cat."

"Don't worry. Cats are highly effective, even for those who aren't used to them." He straightened. "I have a patient waiting, so we need to wrap this up." He picked up the pet carrier and placed it on Shuta's lap.

"Wait, what?"

"I'll see you in a week."

The doctor waved his hand, leaving no room for further discussion.

Shuta stepped out of the examination room confused. It felt as though the doctor had forced him to leave. And the sofa in the waiting room was empty. He was standing frozen in bafflement when he noticed a pale hand beckoning to him from the reception window.

"Mr. Kagawa, this way, please."

This feels like some kind of movie set. He looked around nervously for any hidden cameras. Then he made his way to the window, where the nurse was peering out at him.

"Please pass me the prescription form."

Shuta did as he was told and watched as the nurse disappeared from the reception window.

The carrier shook unsteadily. It was extremely heavy, altogether a weird sensation for Shuta, who had not held a living creature since the days of classroom rabbits in elementary school. His admiration for the cat's surprisingly calm demeanor brought a smile to his face.

The nurse returned with a paper bag. "Here you go." She thrust it through the window. He shifted the pet carrier into one hand and grabbed the bag. The cat slid across the tilted carrier.

"Oops, sorry," Shuta said to the cat. Then, to the nurse, "Excuse me—what's in this bag? It's quite heavy."

"Supplies. There's also a leaflet with instructions, which I advise you to read carefully." In her mouth, the Kyoto dialect, typically known for its seductive lilt, sounded cold and aloof.

Shuta took a look in the bag and saw plastic bowls, a tray, and a pack of what appeared to be cat food—all essential items for looking after a cat. What an incredibly elaborate setup. This level of detail made Shuta feel uneasy.

"So we're continuing with this charade. Isn't this a bit too much?"

"If you have any questions, please ask the doctor. Take care." The nurse dropped her gaze to her work.

"Excuse me—"

"Take care."

"Um—"

"Take care."

Shuta exited the clinic carrying the bag and pet carrier. It was a challenge to open the door with both hands full.

What in the world just happened?

At the end of the corridor, Shuta saw a man glaring at him. He looked as though he was about to ask him a question. Then he passed Shuta and opened the door to the unit next to the clinic.

It was an awkward task to navigate the stairs without tipping up the pet carrier. Once he stepped outside, he was hit with the moldy stench of the alleyway. It was the scent of reality. The burden in his arms was also all too real.

Shuta's colleague had told him that this was a great clinic. The colleague had heard that from his brother, who had heard it from his wife, who had heard it from her cousin, who had . . . As rumors passed from one person to another, they transformed. He took one step, then another, but the sketch didn't end. The nurse didn't come running after him, and a director didn't call out "Cut!" He was the victim of either some unspeakable medical malpractice or a ridiculous scam.

And here he was, a sick man, holding a cat. He found himself chuckling, his laughter echoing into the distance.

Transporting this living creature proved to be a challenge. Shuta couldn't traverse the crosswalk quickly enough, and it wasn't as if he could balance the carrier on his shoulder either. It took him more than thirty minutes to make it back to his apartment, and all the while the cat squirmed uncomfortably and his arms ached.

When Shuta finally placed the carrier on the floor, the cat seemed to sense it was no longer in motion and began to thrash about, rocking the carrier from side to side. Shuta opened the door, feeling sorry for the poor thing, but the cat didn't emerge.

"What's the matter, cat? You can come out now."

The cat remained out of sight. Worried, Shuta peeked into the carrier and saw it cowering in the back.

What's going on? Shuta rifled through the paper bag. He found two bowls of the same size and the packet of cat food, which made a rustling sound when he shook it. Dry kibble, it seemed.

"For now let's go with water."

He filled one of the bowls with tap water and placed it before the pet carrier. The cat still didn't emerge.

"Oh, wait. The instructions."

Keeping an eye on the carrier, Shuta scanned the leaflet.

> NAME: Bee. Female. Estimated to be 8 years old. Mixed breed. Feed moderate amounts of cat food in the morning and at night. Water bowl must always be full. Clean kitty litter as needed. Generally independent and can be left alone. Small items that can be swallowed and breakable items such as plates and cups should be stowed away in a cupboard. Keep an eye on potted plants. Do not let the cat wander out of the house. That's all.

Shuta reread the instructions, but there wasn't much detail.

"Oh, man. I've never had a cat before. I don't know if I can take care of one for a whole week."

How will the cat use this tray and cat litter? Will she instinctively know how to do her business in it without making a mess in the room? How much do I feed her? Will she scratch the walls?

Shuta was beginning to feel overwhelmed, but there was nobody he could turn to for guidance. He would have to do some research online. At least he knew the cat's name.

He crawled on the floor, looked into the carrier, and was met with a pair of golden eyes.

"Bee," he said. "Hey, come on out here, Bee. You're a girl, aren't you? You must be hungry. Let me feed you."

It was evening, dinnertime for humans, and therefore, it must also be dinnertime for cats. As Shuta absorbed the information on the back of the cat food bag and browsed the Internet to find the correct portion size, he noticed the cat poke its head out.

"Oh! Here she comes."

But the cat quickly withdrew. Shuta's voice had startled her. He held his breath, and after a while the cat stuck half her head out again. She looked up at Shuta. They continued to stare at each other in a silent battle of wills. Was the cat being cautious, or was she testing him? Shuta's legs were tingling from sitting in an awkward position, but he toughed it out with a little shiver.

Finally, a single limb appeared from the carrier, her paw hovering over the floor.

Please come out. My legs are pins and needles.

Just when Shuta was about to reach his breaking point, the cat gently lowered her forepaw. As she pressed her round foot against the floor, a crease formed above her ankle, resembling the chubby wrist of a baby. *Adorable.* She took one step, then another, and finally, her long tail slipped out.

This cat is surprisingly big. That was Shuta's first thought. Bee wasn't large, but he'd imagined cats to be much leaner, like the ones he'd seen in videos squeezing through narrow gaps between walls. This particular cat looked like a fluffy gray blanket. If she tried to squeeze into a crevice, the blanket would spill out.

Shuta gritted his teeth and stretched his legs slowly, so as not to startle the cat by standing up too quickly. He watched as the cat approached the water bowl. After sniffing the bowl, she began lapping up the water.

Shuta rubbed his numb legs and contemplated the cat in wonder. The soft sound of splashing water had never been heard before in this room. Having let her guard down, the cat glanced around. Her gaze landed on the unopened bag of cat food.

"Aha! Okay, hold on a second."

After water, food. The cat was rather easy to read. Shuta opened the bag of cat food and poured some into the other container. The cat sat politely, observing the kibble rattle into the bowl. He'd been sure that the cat would pounce, but she stayed put and watched him with her round eyes, pupils dilated.

"Eat. It looks delicious. Go on."

Shuta picked up a piece of kibble—it looked much like a human snack—and pretended to munch on it. The cat did not move an inch and threw him a look like, *What is this guy doing?*

Feeling like an idiot, Shuta lay back on his bed. He followed the cat's movements out of the corner of his eye, while pretending not to. Eventually, the cat crept closer to the food bowl and began to eat.

The room was filled with a soft crunching sound.

Bee had a large presence, but her movements were quiet. As Shuta lay there, he wondered if this was what all cats were like.

It felt strange to have a cat in this room, where he normally lived alone. As he took a fresh look at his space, he noticed the jumbled mess. Manga and video games were littered about since god knew when. On weekdays, he came home only to sleep, and even on his days off, he slept until noon. It wasn't as if he lacked things, but his home simply offered no joy. There was nary a potted plant in his apartment. If there had been one, it would have died long ago.

For the first time in ages, Shuta tidied his room. He picked up the plastic bottle caps and disposable chopsticks from his convenience store takeout containers scattered on the floor and threw them away. He moved the clothing and magazines to a corner. It had been a long time since he'd done much other than hop from psychiatrist to psychiatrist. The simple act of cleaning his room was oddly invigorating.

He spotted something on the table and made a dive for it. "Oh, this is the kind of thing the leaflet warned about."

The sleeping pills instantly turned into hazardous items. He gathered them up and stashed them in a drawer.

Bee had finished eating and was strolling around the room, sniffing every nook and cranny. She had an easy, light gait. There was something comforting about watching a cat going about on a little adventure.

Where do cats sleep? The clinic hadn't provided him with a cat bed. *It's not cold, but I might leave a fleece blanket out for her. Maybe she'll crawl into my bed.*

As Shuta lost himself in thought, time slipped away. Before he knew it, he had drifted off to sleep without needing to take his medication.

A few days later, Shuta was clutching the pet carrier in his arms and sprinting to the fifth floor. He burst into Nakagyō Kokoro Clinic for the Soul and breathlessly pushed the carrier through the small reception window where the unfriendly nurse from the last visit was sitting.

"Here. The cat. I want to speak with the doctor about it."

"Mr. Kagawa, your appointment is in four days. You still have four days' worth of the cat left."

"No, I do not. I am. Done with it." His shortness of breath was making it difficult for him to speak. "I just want to see the doctor. I'm happy to wait."

"Then, please head to the examination room."

"What, immediately? As I said, I'll wait."

"Please head to the examination room." The nurse shifted her attention to a different task.

Shuta was flabbergasted. After dashing from his office to his apartment, he had placed the cat back in the carrier and rushed over to the clinic. He needed to vent his anger in order to feel some relief. Being seen by the doctor so quickly felt anticlimactic.

"Excuse me?" said Shuta.

"Please wait in the examination room," the nurse said coolly.

Shuta picked up the pet carrier and made his way past the sofa in the waiting room before settling into the cramped examination room.

He felt the weight of the carrier pressing into his lap. The cat couldn't seem to sit still. He knew it wasn't the cat's fault, but still, he was seething. The curtains flew open and the doctor appeared.

"Oh, Mr. Kagawa. You're back. What brings you around today?"

When Shuta saw the doctor's good-natured smile, he exploded. "I've been fired! From my job! Because of this, this cat!"

He clutched the edge of the carrier. The cat must have sensed the tension, for she hissed threateningly inside the carrier.

"Well, that's good to hear," the doctor said, laughing a little.

Shuta's eyes widened.

"G-good to hear?"

"Didn't you want to quit your job? You've solved your problem. I knew this cat was right for you. She's very effective."

The doctor beamed with satisfaction while Shuta tried to regain his composure.

Nope. It's stupid even to be taking this seriously. In the first place, I haven't been treated for anything. But I should at least make my grievances known.

Shuta lifted the carrier from his lap and placed it on the desk.

"I never wanted to quit my job. I came to you for help because I *didn't* want to leave. It's a prestigious company!"

The doctor tilted his head.

"Did you not say working for your company was like working at a sweatshop?"

"All companies are like that. No company, large or small, is perfect."

Shuta was astonished with himself for defending his lousy company. But this was what his friends had told him. *It's the same everywhere. At least you're being well paid. You're asking for too much,* they'd said. So he'd told himself the same and had held out somehow. He felt depressed just thinking about it.

"It's downright unfair. I was fired, just like that. What was the point of putting up with everything all this time?"

"Well . . ." The doctor looked at his watch. "My next patient hasn't shown up yet. If you want to talk, I'm all ears."

Shuta felt exhausted all of a sudden. This clinic was unlike any other. His cries of pain and tears did not even earn a superficial show of sympathy. But maybe this was preferable to a hollow pretense of concern. An inscrutable smile adorned the doctor's face as he sat, legs crossed in front of him.

"There were no issues when I first brought the cat home," explained Shuta. "Bee slept soundly. I fed her breakfast in the morning and went to work as usual."

Yes. It had been only that first night Bee had provided

solace. After that, it was a repeat of the usual. A toxic workplace wasn't so simple for a cat to fix.

Cats were unexpectedly straightforward.

Shuta had smiled as he observed Bee eating her food. He'd wondered if he would wake up to find the room in utter chaos, but such concerns proved groundless. Shuta had found the cat curled up under the table. She hadn't been up to any mischief. When Shuta got up, Bee immediately came over to him. *Has she already grown attached to me after only one day? Or is she trained to be that way?*

As he made his way to the bathroom, he noticed the cat trailing behind him.

"What's up? Do you want some food?"

He looked down at Bee, who was rubbing her head against his shin. With her triangular ears flattened against her head, she nuzzled Shuta's leg with surprising strength. Just a few hours ago, Shuta had been afraid to touch the cat for fear of being scratched, but he couldn't ignore her now that she was being so affectionate.

He touched Bee's forehead with his fingers and found it silky. *What a peculiar texture.* He'd imagined the cat to have fur like fine bristles on a hairbrush, but the reality was entirely different. As the cat looked up, their eyes met, and he instinctively retracted his hand in concern. But the cat stretched her neck and pressed her cheek against him, then burrowed more insistently into Shuta's palm.

"Wow, you're so soft and fluffy."

But she wasn't floppy like a stuffed animal. She was firm and solid under his hand. *What does she feel like? A fluffy . . . tennis ball?*

Her fur looked short, but her coat was thick enough to run his hand through it. Her undercoat was downy and white. Upon closer inspection, her topcoat, which had looked plain gray yesterday, revealed a subtle blend of brown that formed a gentle marbled pattern.

What a beauty you are.

Bee pressed gently but persistently until he gave her more pets. After a few moments on his hands and knees, he went to prepare her food and water before attending to his own needs. It seemed that having a pet disrupted the flow of one's daily routine.

"Maybe it's not such a bad thing."

Shuta crouched down on his elbows to observe Bee up close as she ate. Thanks to a restful night's sleep, he felt lighter than he had in a long time. But the desire to avoid going to work lingered.

But if I can make it through today . . .

That was his morning mantra. If he could get through today, tomorrow would be easier. He wasn't going to quit.

As Bee lapped at her water, he scratched her head, and her eyes fluttered shut as if she was basking in bliss. It truly felt like if he could just get through today, he would find his way.

"Mamiya has been at the bottom of our department for three weeks in a row. A round of applause for him, please!" Emoto's husky voice echoed across the floor. Shuta felt his stomach flip as sparse hand-clapping broke out. It was a ritual to use the weekly morning meeting as a stage for public shaming. From behind his desk, Emoto, the department manager, was giving Mamiya a roasting in front of this team.

"He's dragging all of us down. No matter how much we hustle, our department can't hit our target numbers, all thanks to this guy. Living the dream, huh, Mamiya? Cashing paychecks while kicking back."

Emoto, an Osaka native, spoke in the Kansai dialect instead of standard Japanese, even in professional settings.

Mamiya kept his head down and remained silent. None of the sales team members dared look him in the eye. Being called out in front was enough to shatter your spirit.

Witnessing someone else get chewed out was stomach turning.

"Hey, Kagawa!"

Shuta flinched. "Y-yes?"

"You're not far behind," said Emoto. "How do you guys even dare to show your faces at work? If it was me, I would've quit a long time ago out of shame."

Shuta clenched his fists. He'd learned that in these situations it was better to force a wry smile than to hang his head. He let out a nervous chuckle.

"You think this is a joke? Are you an idiot?" asked Emoto. "Usually, scrawny, pasty guys aren't cut out for this work. Good salespeople are tanned from working outside the office. Look at me. This is a real man's arm."

Emoto revealed his nicely bronzed forearms. Shuta suspected it might be a golf tan, given how the arm was pale from the wrist down, but he kept his suspicions to himself. He laughed weakly.

Emoto clicked his tongue and walked over to someone else.

"You're not thinking about asking for overtime, are you? With subpar performances like yours, I'm amazed you're trying to squeeze the company for more money. Have you thought about the importance of contributing to the success of our company?"

Emoto berated everyone who didn't have a strong sales record. He was known to smack people on the head with bundles of paper or with ballpoint pens. Nothing was more excruciatingly embarassing. Shuta had been singled out before the team several times, and each time he'd shaken with shame. After he was offered up as a living sacrifice, people avoided speaking to him for a while—no words seemed adequate.

The air was shot through with fear—anyone could be next. Emoto was notorious for being a power-abusing manager, but there were others like him scattered across different departments. In the sales department, employees who fell short of their quotas were essentially stripped of their human rights. Those who couldn't stand it quit.

Shuta had completed his off-site meetings but hadn't managed to bring in much new business that day. An elderly man had patiently listened to his long spiel, but ultimately, Shuta couldn't convince him to invest any more. Clients rarely purchased financial products during these sales visits, especially when conducted by junior salespeople like Shuta, who were almost always turned away at the door.

After joining the brokerage firm, Shuta learned that finance was all about collecting commission from customers. If you were lucky, the value of the products you recommended would increase, and the client would thank you. But it wasn't your job to make your customers any profit. The goal was to make them deposit more and more money.

The firm was located at the intersection of Karasuma and Shijō streets, an area teeming with people and jam-packed with banks, department stores, and other commercial buildings. When Shuta had first arrived in Kyoto, he'd been excited to work in such a prime location filled with skyscrapers. Now he lumbered through the streets, his painfully heavy gait drawing stares from passing tourists.

Shuta knew that as soon as he returned to his desk that day, Emoto was going to call on him, and he would have to report on his performance. He was probably going to be yelled at again. As he trudged down the street, someone tapped him on the shoulder.

It was his colleague Kijima. He, too, looked tired.

"Hey, Kagawa. Perfect timing. I've been wanting to catch up with you."

Kijima also worked in the sales department. He was around Shuta's age and was similarly mild-mannered. In the past, they'd both been underachievers and had frequently griped about work together. But lately, Kijima had begun to win bigger clients and no longer competed for the bottom spot.

They dropped into a coffee shop close to work. Shuta was relieved to have reason to take a detour. He'd been dragging his feet in everything lately.

"What happened to Mamiya today was awful, wasn't it?" muttered Kijima.

"Yeah, that guy's been a target lately. It's uncomfortable to watch," said Shuta, but deep down, he knew it was better to watch than to be attacked. He was grateful for Mamiya. Without him, Shuta would be the one forced to stand before everyone.

"You've been so lucky, Kijima. You've been doing great. You need to tell me how you're selling products with such low interest rates."

Shuta couldn't stop himself from making the snide remark. There was no point in learning new sales strategies now. He'd been through countless in-house training and role-playing sessions. The truth was this: successful salespeople possessed unique talent that set them apart from the rest. When companies ignored this fact and imposed the same quota on everyone, workplaces became toxic. Kijima, too, had complained about this until recently. But something felt different today.

Kijima cracked a smile.

"I'm quitting," he said.

"Whaaat?"

"Here, this is for you."

Kijima opened his briefcase and took out an envelope stuffed with papers.

"What are these?"

"Documents that need to be given to our manager Emoto's clients—income and expenditure reports, payment statements, receipts, and the like. They're organized by client, so distribute them according to the list."

"No, no, no. This is all wrong." Shuta's face contorted as he looked at the documents. "We're strictly forbidden from handing statements directly to clients. And look at this." His face twitched as he examined one of the documents. "This is a receipt. This isn't a document the sales team should be casually handing out. I'm pretty sure it needs to be issued from the collections department or some other department that specializes in processing payments . . . to prevent fraud." Shuta fell silent and broke out into a cold sweat.

A smile flickered on Kijima's lips.

"I don't get it myself, but according to Emoto, he has a special contact in the collections department and was granted authorization to issue receipts. He's on a different level in his career than us grunts, so he said not to sweat the small stuff."

"Is that right?" asked Shuta.

"That's what I've been told."

Kijima laughed coolly.

Shuta had never heard of such a thing, but he accepted that as a lower-ranking employee there were countless things he didn't know, far outnumbering what he did.

"Well, if Emoto says so, I guess he must be right."

"The people on the list are our loyal and valued clients. I just meet with them from time to time, and they throw some new business opportunities my way. It's an easy job," said Kijima.

"If it's such a sweet gig, why are you giving it to me? Why are you even quitting? You've got an impressive sales record."

"Remember how I used to stand in front of everyone during those morning meetings every week? Emoto said I was the dumbest employee to have ever walked on the face of the earth." Kijima let out an embarrassed chuckle.

Shuta wasn't sure how to react. Things had been exactly as Kijima described. And since he'd brought it up himself, Shuta could only nod in agreement.

"Yeah."

"Just when I thought I was at my wit's end, Emoto told me he was going to give me some of his clients. I was astonished that he would offer such a thing, but at the time, all I could think about was escaping from the morning meetings. I figured it wasn't a big deal if all I had to do was deliver documents. Most of his clients are elderly, so I just have to make small talk with them when I drop by. Even today, I spent the morning visiting one of Emoto's clients—a sweet old lady who looks forward to my visits."

"There are good clients like that, aren't there?" said Shuta.

"The lady remembered that I'm from Shikoku and went out of her way to prepare sweets from my hometown. While I ate them, she said, 'Your parents must be so happy you work for such a prestigious company. You're a perfect son.'"

Shuta felt like he'd been stabbed in the heart.

Kijima laughed at his speechlessness.

"At that moment, a thought came to me. *I'm no perfect son. I'm so bad at my job that I can't even stand up to my boss.* Then, suddenly, I felt like an idiot for trying so hard to hold on. I thought, *I should quit now. I'm not going back. If I go back, it'll be the same thing all over again.*" Kijima stood up. His clouded eyes were now clear. "I bet these files will be handed to Mamiya next. He's in a lot of trouble and won't be able to refuse."

"Wait. I don't want to do this."

"Kagawa, you might appear meek, but unlike Mamiya or me in the past, you know you can't keep going like this. I'm sure you have the courage to stand up to him."

As Shuta sat there gawping, Kijima walked out of the coffee shop, leaving the documents on the table. Shuta didn't know what to do, but he couldn't leave them there. He stuffed the papers back into the envelope, tucked it into his briefcase, and headed back to the office.

When Emoto called on him, as always, Shuta was visibly distracted. Emoto gave an irritated click of his tongue.

"Hey, can't you at least pretend to be motivated? And what's up with Kijima? Can't young people these days come back to the office according to schedule?"

It was long past closing time, but, as a matter of course, many were still in the office, working overtime for free. Shuta was restless. Hours passed, but Kijima didn't come back.

"Hey. Someone call Kijima. How many hours does it take for him to visit a client?" shouted Emoto.

Everyone exchanged knowing looks. Someone on the team made the call, but no matter how many times they called, Kijima didn't pick up. Eventually, a frustrated Emoto called Kijima himself. Still no answer.

Shuta watched Emoto seethe with rage. *Is Kijima serious about not coming back?* He gently nudged the briefcase of documents by his feet further under his desk.

When Kijima continued not to pick up, Emoto called

him on his personal phone. Still no response. The team members were giving Emoto strange looks. Normally, their manager wasn't the type to make a fuss over a team member not returning to the office.

Shuta quietly slipped out. His apartment building was near Kyoto City Hall and he usually took the subway, but he wanted some time to think, so he decided to walk home.

The best course of action is to return the documents to Kijima somehow. If that's not possible, I'll go to work early tomorrow morning and sneak them onto Emoto's desk. The worst thing would be to take Kijima's place and go round to the clients on the list. I don't want anything to do with this. How did I end up in this position?

Frowning, he opened the door to his apartment. Bee sat waiting. She let out a soft meow.

"Oh no! I'm so sorry. I forgot all about you."

Shuta dropped the briefcase in the doorway and crouched down. When he reached out, Bee walked up to his hand, closed her eyes, and nuzzled her head against his palm.

"I'm so sorry, Bee. I was planning to come home to you earlier."

Bee's water bowl was empty. Shuta bit his lip. He had really messed up. With his jacket still on, he filled her water and food bowls. Then he watched for a while as she ate.

"I can't even look after just one cat . . . And you waited so patiently without even complaining. You're a better soul than me."

The furniture and walls showed no signs of damage or scratching. The thought that Bee had been a good girl, waiting for him without getting into any mischief, brought a lump to Shuta's throat.

There was a faint electronic sound. His phone was ringing, but it wasn't in his pocket.

"Right," he muttered as he rifled through his briefcase. He'd hastily transferred everything from his desk into it before he fled the office.

It was his mother.

"Hello, Mom." Shuta's chest tightened at the sound of his mother's voice. "No, I'm already home. I just got back . . . Yeah, no, I ate. Don't worry."

The phone calls from his mother were always the same. They never had anything important to discuss, and Shuta always gave the same answers.

"I've told you many times before: I'm not a midcareer recruit. I'm a recent college graduate with one previous job under my belt. We're more valuable than recent grads with no experience. That's how things are now."

His mother was always worried about how Shuta was doing. After graduating from college, Shuta had secured a position at a medium-sized food company in his hometown. But he was assigned to work at a remote factory far away, where he was severely bullied, leading him to quit his job within six months. He remembered the shock of encountering the first major setback of his life.

He also remembered the disappointed faces of his parents, especially his father's. Although his father didn't express it in words, he must have been disappointed that his son, whom he'd sent to college, had so quickly become unemployed.

That was why he had been thrilled when he found a job at his current company, which was more prestigious than his last. He was able to save face with his parents. At least, that's what he believed.

"It's okay. Don't worry. My current workplace is different from my old one. It's a big-name company. Whole different league." He gave a small, dry laugh. "They're expecting a lot from me. Today, at the morning meeting, my supervisor said I was within striking distance of the top spot . . . Hmm? . . . No, it's not great. Everyone else is also close to the top. Everyone's doing their best."

Everyone's doing their best.

Everyone's doing their best.

He paused to keep his voice from shaking. *Everyone's doing their best. It's not like I can't do my best, too.*

He ended the call. Bee had finished eating and was wiping her mouth with a paw. Then she started licking it.

Is scrubbing a paw with a tongue right after a meal an effective way to clean it?

A small smile crept across Shuta's face. After carefully cleaning her paw, Bee began stroking her face with it. She took her time, wiping her face gently and thoroughly. The way she rubbed her eyes was almost humanlike. When she was done, she seemed content.

"It must be nice to be a cat with not a care in the world."

Bee sat quietly as Shuta stroked her around the cheeks. The moment Shuta removed his hand, Bee licked her paw again and scrubbed herself more vigorously than before. It was as if she was displeased with how he'd messed up her hairdo.

"Excuse me! How rude. Okay, I'm going to rough up your fur even more."

The cat gracefully evaded his outstretched hand and stepped away for further grooming.

"I'm sorry. I won't do it again. Please come back."

Bee kept her distance, clearly uninterested in his attempts to win her over. Shuta laughed out loud. It had been a long time since he'd laughed genuinely and not as a way to mask his true feelings. For a moment, he forgot the burden Kijima had forced upon him.

It must be because of Bee.

If he could get through today, things actually might be easier tomorrow. He believed it.

Shuta heard a sound in the distance. *Oh, right,* he thought as he half opened his eyes. He'd set his alarm for earlier than usual, hoping to get to work early today. But alongside the high-pitched ringing, he heard another odd noise—scratching and tearing.

He chuckled to himself. *Tinnitus first thing in the morning?* But then a sharp ripping sound jolted him from bed.

Confetti! All over the room. *What is this?* As he stood in disbelief, he heard more ripping sounds. In the corner, Bee was skillfully holding a piece of paper with her front paw and tearing it apart with her teeth.

"Bee, what are you doing?" The cat looked up at Shuta with the paper still in her mouth. A profit-and-loss report lay in shreds.

One of the documents he had planned to return secretly today. Bee clawed at it as if to show off her work.

"*How . . . how* did this happen?"

He had not removed any documents from the envelope the previous night. He looked over at the briefcase, noticed that the flap was open, likely from when he'd taken his phone out. It seemed the cat had fished the envelope out of his briefcase.

With a purr, Bee pressed her soft body against his leg. Silky fur through the thin fabric of his pajamas. Even amidst the shards of paper, she moved gracefully, her footfalls silent.

Shuta snuck into the office, hoping to find Yuina Sakashita. He had first met Yuina at an office gathering in which they had been seated next to each other, and she was the only person he knew in accounting. He made his way to her department and prayed she was in.

It was still early, so there were few people in the office. Shuta was relieved to find Yuina among them. He called her over quietly, and thankfully, she remembered him.

"You're Shuta from sales, right? What's up?"

"I have the favor of a lifetime to ask you. I need your help."

When Shuta showed her the torn documents, Yuina's eyes widened. "What— Are these client receipts?"

"They're my manager Emoto's clients. He said he got special authorization from the collections department to issue statements for the clients on this list."

The list was the only document that had mercifully

escaped the cat's claws. Yuina quirked an eyebrow as she scrutinized it.

"There are so many people on this list. You're telling me the sales team is handing receipts directly to these clients? That's impossible. Also, why are all these documents torn?"

To dispel her suspicions, Shuta explained the situation honestly, but he kept Kijima out of it. He brought his hands together and bowed deeply.

"Please reissue the receipts without telling Emoto."

"Whaat? I can't do that," said Yuina. "I can't release customer documents without proper approval. I can't hand them to a sales representative, not with a verbal request like this."

"But I heard that Emoto has special authorization. The people on the list are longtime VIP customers, so there must be some way to process their paperwork that we're unaware of."

"Um, I don't think so."

Suspicion clouded Yuina's face.

"If my boss finds out, he's going to kill me. He's a total monster. Can you please help me and reissue the documents discreetly? I beg you."

Shuta pleaded until Yuina reluctantly gave in.

"I'll check to see if there are any records of these

receipts being issued. Maybe there's an internal policy or rule I'm unaware of."

"Right," said Shuta, relieved. "After all, this sweatshop of a firm doesn't even pay for overtime."

Yuina threw him a sarcastic eye roll. "All corporations are sweatshops," she said before heading back to her desk.

The problem was far from being resolved, but Shuta saw a glimmer of hope. He had a good feeling about Yuina. She was reliable and was sure to be helpful. Even if things didn't work out, he was going to find a way to thank her.

Shuta headed directly to his client appointment in the morning and returned to the sales department in the afternoon. Emoto was sitting at his desk, taciturn and displeased. His silence was concerning, but no one dared to approach him. Shuta, too, pretended not to notice anything.

In the evening, just as he was heading to the accounting department to see how things were progressing, he felt someone yank his shirt from behind and drag him toward the landing of the emergency staircase. Shuta gulped. It was Emoto.

"O-oh, hey."

"What the *hell* do you think you're doing?"

Emoto's face had turned ashen; spittle spewed from the corner of his mouth. There was a nastiness to his tone, different from his usual bluster.

"You asked the accounting department to reissue the documents? You've *got* to be KIDDING ME!"

In Emoto's hand was the crumpled list.

He knows everything. Shuta felt his knees buckle.

"I'm really sorry. I was careless and damaged some important client documents," said Shuta.

"I don't care about that! Why do you even have this? What happened to Kijima?" Emoto's mouth was at Shuta's ear. It felt like his eardrum was going to burst.

"He's . . ." Shuta had no idea that Emoto would be so livid. He didn't even know where to begin his explanation. All he felt was fear. "Kijima left these documents with me and . . . quit. He's not coming back."

Emoto stood open-mouthed. His gaze roved around his feet as if searching for something. Then he jerked his head up. "*You* should quit."

"What?"

"Quit. Right now. Like Kijima. See, useless salespeople like you are a liability for the company. I'll take care of the paperwork. Normally, you'd be dismissed on disciplinary grounds for losing important documents, but I'll let you go on your own terms. Okay?"

Emoto was smiling, but his eyes were bloodshot.

Shuta tried to explain. "I didn't lose the documents. Actually, my cat was being mischievous and—"

"I don't care!" Emoto's voice echoed through the stairwell. He grabbed Shuta by the collar of his shirt, making him choke. "You're fired! Someone like you who forges documents deserves to be fired!"

"Wh-what?"

"We have proof that you requested fraudulent documents from the accounting department. You and Kijima were in on it; you tried to cheat our clients. We have all the evidence we need."

The word "fired" hit him like a ton of bricks. *What is he talking about?*

"Don't underestimate what I'll do. I'll make sure you're fired, no matter what. We'll be better off without people like you around. You're fired! Fired! Fired!"

Shuta turned his back and scampered down the stairs, until he could no longer hear the yelling and cursing. *I have to get out of here right now.* That was his sole thought.

There was a soft *meow* from the pet carrier perched on the desk in the examination room.

Shuta just couldn't be in that place a moment longer.

After Emoto's violent harangue, he ran out of the office, went straight to his apartment, and forced the cat into the carrier. The cat had no clue what had hit her. He was also clueless. Instead of seeking answers, he prioritized protecting his vulnerable heart.

"Hmm." The doctor folded his arms and sat back. "I see."

"I don't get it. Out of nowhere, he started screaming, 'Fired! Fired!' Yes, I messed up and ruined important company documents, but I didn't expect him to explode like that."

Shuta was regaining his composure. Perhaps it had been inappropriate for him to have rushed over to the clinic. He felt a little embarrassed.

"Hmm," the doctor murmured again. "I don't know much about the corporate world, but I don't think it's that simple to fire someone, do you? Ah, Chitose, please take this cat with you."

The doctor was addressing the nurse, who had just come in. With a stony expression, she took hold of the carrier and disappeared into the back. Shuta felt a sudden pang of loss, but he quickly brushed it aside.

"At a normal company, it probably isn't," he said. "But at my firm they're more likely to push employees to resign rather than take extended leaves of absence, even for mental health reasons. Given Emoto's position, I could potentially face dismissal based on disciplinary grounds. If that happens, it could ruin my chances of finding another job."

"I see. Well, don't worry too much about it. Now, if you have nothing else to discuss, I have a client coming soon." The doctor smiled and gestured at the door.

Shuta's anger began to resurface. "Excuse me, doctor. Were you listening? I've been fired from my job because your cat tore up my documents. You're acting like it has nothing to do with you. How are you going to take responsibility for this?"

"Responsibility? I don't know what on earth you mean. Are you saying you want to return to that sweatshop-like company?"

"Huh?"

Is that what I want? If he returned, would he be able to start over at that office? Wouldn't it just be the same thing all over again, as Kijima had said? He couldn't tell his parents what had happened. How could he, when he had, just yesterday, said to them that there was nothing to worry about? Shuta stared darkly at his clenched fists in his lap.

"I don't want to go back. At this point, I don't care where I work. Please, just help me find a job."

"I completely understand," said the doctor. "Okay, we'll prescribe you a cat." The doctor turned around and called out toward the curtains. "Chitose, can you bring me the cat?"

The nurse appeared with the pet carrier. "Dr. Nikké, are you sure he's the right person for this?" she asked a little skeptically.

"Yes, yes. It's all good," the doctor said. "You worry too much, Chitose."

"Well, don't say I didn't warn you," she replied brusquely before positioning the carrier on the desk and leaving.

The balance of power between the nurse and doctor seemed quite equal; if anything, the nurse might hold more authority, Shuta observed.

Seeing some concern in Shuta's eyes, the doctor gave a strained laugh. "She's always scolding me for being unreliable. She's generally kind. Runs hot and cold, as they say."

"I see."

The doctor seemed friendly, mild-mannered, and Shuta trusted him. *No hidden skeletons in his closet. Is he married? Maybe he's dating that classic beauty of a nurse.* With such thoughts on his mind, his eyes wandered to the carrier perched on the desk. Shuta blinked.

"This is the same one, isn't it?"

The gray-furred, golden-eyed Bee looked up at him from the carrier.

"Correct. You've had no adverse reactions so far, so let's

run with the same cat for a while and see how it goes. I'll give you a ten-day supply this time. If she doesn't suit you, please contact me even if you're not done with the prescription."

"Excuse me?"

"Yes?"

"So . . . I'm taking the same cat?" asked Shuta.

The doctor peered curiously through the door of the carrier.

"Do you want a bigger cat?"

"Um, no, this one's fine."

"Well, take care, then. Oh! Don't forget to pick up the rest of your prescription from reception before you leave."

Shuta felt he had been driven out of the examination room all over again. At the reception window, the nurse awaited him with her surly look.

"Here are the supplies. You'll find a leaflet with instructions inside. Please make sure to read it carefully."

Along with a package of food and kitty litter, inside the bag was a piece of corrugated cardboard. Shuta looked up at the nurse, a question forming in his gaze. *Is the cardboard meant for scratching?*

"If that scratching pad breaks or the cat doesn't seem to like it, please replace it for her."

"I have to buy it myself?"

There was something else in the bag—a small orange collar about the size of Shuta's wrist. And a length of some kind of cord. A leash, perhaps. Everything was brand-new.

"Um, is this—"

"Please read the instruction leaflet."

"Well, this—"

"The leaflet?"

"Okay."

Pet carrier and paper bag in hand, Shuta left the clinic. He took the leaflet out of the bag, wondering what it might say this time.

> **NAME:** Bee. Female. Estimated to be 8 years old. Mixed breed. Feed moderate amounts of cat food in the morning and at night. Water bowl must always be full. Clean kitty litter as needed. Please make sure she is wearing her collar and leash when taking her outside. Please let her scratch frequently to relieve stress. Avoid leaving her alone for long periods of time, as it may make her emotionally unstable. That's all.

"Taking her outside." Shuta wondered what it meant. Did it mean he had to walk her on a leash like a dog? He did not want to do that. Even just putting a collar on her seemed cruel.

As he stepped out of the building and glanced up from the alleyway, he noticed the sky had already turned dark.

"Bee," Shuta called out to the cat.

She was looking back at him. The weight in his arm was becoming familiar.

It was probably because he had left the building in a daze, but he soon realized he was strolling along a street in the opposite direction of his apartment. Ahead of him was Nishiki Market, the shopping arcade on Nishikikōji Street. As he approached the market, the cat began to thrash around inside the carrier, possibly unsettled by the heavy pedestrian traffic and the aromas emanating from the food stalls.

He decided not to go into the arcade and headed north. As he was walking along Rokkaku Street he heard the loud tolling of the temple bell of Rokkakudo. The carrier rattled again and the startled cat meowed loudly. Shuta had no choice but to turn eastward again, away from the noise.

Feeling disoriented, he began to walk in random directions. The streets around here were laid out in a grid, so he knew that if he kept walking in a straight line, he would eventually hit a thoroughfare.

After a few minutes, he spotted a convenience store at

the end of the street. Shuta had never been to this one before, as it wasn't on his usual route. He decided to go in since he had no food at his apartment and the cat was sitting quietly in her carrier.

Nothing on the bento display shelves appealed to him. He had no appetite. He had no job. He was going to run out of money soon. And he had no girlfriend.

Yuina Sakashita, whom he'd talked to that morning, popped into his head. He didn't blame her for what had happened, but he wanted to ask her why she'd handed the list to Emoto. Once things settled down, he might ask her to dinner. Shuta laughed at his own nonchalant attitude.

A young man passing by gave him a look. "Hey! What are you laughing at?" he asked.

The man was dressed in workwear and wore a towel around his head. He had an air of trouble about him.

Better stay away from him. Shuta quickly turned toward the exit. At that moment, the door of the carrier in Shuta's hand swung open, and the cat leaped out.

"Huh?"

The cat landed neatly on the convenience store floor, her paws making no sound. A customer entered the store through the automatic door, and the cat slid out between his legs. It all happened in a matter of seconds.

"Bee!"

Shuta hurried out after her, but the cat was nowhere to be seen. There were several cars parked in the lot. He dropped to his hands and knees to see if she might be hiding under one.

"This is unbelievable. *Bee*, where are you?"

He heard a little meow. He looked up, and there was Bee, sitting on the hood of a black car. He breathed a sigh of relief.

"Come here."

Just as he reached out to pick her up, she began to scratch the hood vigorously with both front paws.

Shuta gulped. *Nooooo.* His blood ran cold. But what startled him more was the stern voice that came from behind.

"Whoa, whoa, *whoa*!"

It was the man dressed in workwear he'd just seen. He had turned as white as a sheet.

"That's the boss's new car!"

The man sprang forward at the vehicle. Bee jumped up in panic and scampered onto the roof. And there she started to claw at the car again.

"Crap!"

The man looked on the verge of tears as he wiped over the scratches on the hood with his sleeve.

Shuta stood there in a daze. When the cat came back to his feet, he picked her up absentmindedly. "Bee . . ."

"Is that your cat?"

Shuta flinched. He hadn't noticed another man come up beside him. He had a stern expression and was dressed in a somber suit with a thick gold chain that twinkled beneath his collar.

The man in workwear scuttled around the car and bowed deeply. "I'm so sorry, boss. It was that damn cat's fault."

"You fool!" shouted the man in the suit.

Both Shuta and the man in the workwear froze. Passersby stopped to have a look.

"Why are you blaming the cat?"

"I'm so sorry." The man in workwear bowed his head as the other man tutted loudly. He inspected the hood of his car.

"Hey, kid." He addressed Shuta, who remained frozen.

"Y-yes?"

"I'm not one to sweat the small stuff, but this seems like a case of a pet owner being negligent. In other words, it's not the cat's fault but yours. Don't you think so?"

"Uh, yes, I guess."

"All right. You'll have to pay for this. Kōsuke, take this guy to the office."

"Yes, boss." The man in workwear gave Shuta a look.

Office? What sort of office? An office for shady business?

In his mind an image of being brutally roughed up surfaced. *Is this a nightmare?* He had only just lost his job.

Bee felt heavy and warm in his arms. She remained calm, as if without a care in the world. Come to think of it, it had been in the instruction leaflet: *Please make sure she is wearing her collar and leash when taking her outside.* It also mentioned that she needed to scratch frequently to relieve stress. As he looked at the black car, Shuta realized that the collar, leash, and scratching pad had been provided for a reason.

There was a small Shinto altar on the wall. That was about all that caught Shuta's attention. He'd expected to see samurai swords or a yakuza family crest on the wall, but he'd been brought to the office of an ordinary construction company. The parking lot was filled with small excavators and trucks, while men in wide-leg construction wear filed in and out of the office. Shuta sat waiting in the reception area in the corner of the office, Bee's pet carrier resting on his lap.

On the way over, Kōsuke Higuchi had driven them, proudly letting them know that the company owned the building where their office was located. A man of many words, he also told Shuta that his boss had had a tough time convincing his wife to let him buy a new car and that his boss had excitedly counted down the days until his new car arrived. Jinnai, the boss in question, sat in the back seat in grim silence.

"What? You've already messed up the car?" a shrill voice echoed through the office. "Kōsuke! What were you doing?"

Kōsuke looked sheepishly at a woman in glasses and with a frown on her face.

"I'm sorry, Sister Satsuki. That damn cat started scratching out of nowhere."

"Don't blame the cat. You're the one who volunteered to drive the car. And don't call me 'Sister.' It makes me sound like the wife of a yakuza."

"I'm sorry, Sister Satsuki," said Kōsuke with a bow.

The office staff tittered. It seemed Satsuki, the woman in glasses, and middle-aged, was a senior manager at the company.

Jinnai let out a low chuckle. He was reclined on a leather sofa in the back of the office. "What kind of yakuza's wife would be such a tightwad?"

"What did you say?" Satsuki glared at him. "Anyway, who takes the car just for a quick trip to the convenience store? Good grief! You always get so excited when you have something new . . ." Satsuki grumbled, then sat down in front of Shuta.

"Hello. I'm Satsuki Jinnai. I handle accounting for this company."

"I-I'm Shuta Kagawa. I'm very sorry for the trouble I've caused." Shuta bowed. He wondered if this woman was the boss's wife—they shared a last name. When he glanced up at Satsuki, he was met with her icy glare.

"How old are you? You look young, but you're not still in school, are you? Where do you live? Do you have insurance? I'll get an estimate on the cost of repairs and talk to our insurance company. Can you do the same? I don't think it'll cost that much, given it's a new car."

The questions came in rapid succession, and Shuta became slack-jawed. "Well, um . . ."

Satsuki raised an eyebrow. "What do you do? What kind of job makes you dress up in a suit and walk around with a cat?"

"Um, so . . . I don't have a job."

"You don't?"

"I was working for a large company until yesterday, but just today, I was fired—no, I resigned."

"So you're unemployed?"

The way she had so simply stated the truth felt like a stab to Shuta's heart.

A shadow fell over Shuta. When he glanced up, he found Jinnai, the boss, looking down at him.

"There are two things I can't forgive," said Jinnai.

"Oh?"

"First, lazy, young, able-bodied folks who avoid work. They really get under my skin."

"I'm not lazy. Until this morning, I was working at a good company—"

"The other thing!" Jinnai suddenly raised his voice. "People who abuse kitty cats."

"Kitty cats?"

Shuta was taken aback. The cat jostled the carrier. *Is he referring to Bee? And did he think I was abusing her?*

"Yeah, that's right. I won't let anyone get away with mistreating such adorable creatures. I'll beat the hell out of that worthless scum to teach them a lesson."

As Satsuki heard Jinnai raise his voice, her face contorted. "Keep it down, will you?" she said. "Enough with the cats this and that. Mr. Kagawa, was it? Don't worry about this man. He watches too many cat videos and acts like he has a cat."

"Hah!" Jinnai exclaimed testily. "If I was the cat's owner, I wouldn't put it in a cheapo carrier with a door that pops open so easily. I wouldn't take it outside without putting a collar on it in the first place. What if the cat gets lost? Isn't that irresponsible? Am I wrong?"

"I have a collar for her. I was going to put it on her as

soon as we got home," Shuta explained, swiftly pulling the collar out of the paper bag.

When Jinnai saw it, he roared even louder. "It's not even the right size!" He grabbed the paper bag from Shuta and scattered its contents. His eyes widened when he saw the package of cat food. "What the hell is this? Did you even look at the nutrition label? It's loaded with carbohydrates! Don't you know an adult cat needs more animal protein?"

"Protein?" *Cats need protein?* Shuta looked down at the carrier on his lap. He couldn't see the cat because she had tucked herself away in the back. "I don't know much about it. But it's cat food, so I thought it would be fine."

"Fine?" The look in Jinnai's eyes turned increasingly grim. "How old is that cat? It's obviously not a kitten."

"She's certainly not a kitten, but she's not that old either. Oh yeah, the instruction leaflet said she's eight years old. Plus, she ate this food yesterday and seemed to enjoy it."

"Are you a demon?" shouted Jinnai.

Shuta's mouth fell open. Jinnai himself was the one acting like a furious demon.

"Eight? That's a delicate age, when they're just starting to dip their toes into senior cathood, but you're handling it all so irresponsibly. And you were planning to put this tiny collar on her. I don't like this, not one bit!"

"I said keep it down. Look, you've frightened Mr. Kagawa," said Satsuki.

Shuta felt a wave of relief; then he caught the intense, pointed gaze Satsuki was throwing him from behind her spectacles—a stare even sharper than Jinnai's.

"I did a quick estimate for the cost of repair to the car. It's going to be around a million yen," she said.

"A million yen? No way." Shuta laughed bitterly. That was equivalent to several months' rent. He thought Satsuki was joking, but when he saw the looks on the couple's faces, he was alarmed to find that they were dead serious.

"That's impossible. I don't have that kind of money. I just quit my job."

"Well, if that's the case, you'll have to work for us, starting tomorrow," Jinnai said with a hint of warning. "We'll take the cost of repairs from your pay. Work hard, and you'll get a fair wage from us. Give it six months, and you'll be square with your debt."

"Work for you?" echoed Shuta.

The rugged men in workwear and Jinnai, too, were all bigger than Shuta. It was evident that these guys were no strangers to physical labor. Still, Shuta looked up at Jinnai, wondering if perhaps . . .

"Do you need help with accounting or the like?" he asked.

"I want you to work onsite, of course. Get out there and work your ass off," said Jinnai.

"I don't think I can. I don't have any experience with manual labor, and I'm not exactly athletic either."

"Stop whining. You're on the job with us starting tomorrow. Got it?" Jinnai looked down at Shuta and narrowed his eyes.

Shuta gave up. Sure, he'd said he didn't care where he worked. But after all the trouble he'd gone through to escape from a toxic workplace, it seemed like he had ended up somewhere worse.

Bee was shuffling restlessly in circles. He vowed to reread the cat's instruction leaflet, and this time he would make sure not to make a single mistake.

"Hey, you'll hurt your back if you lift stuff like that."

The tanned, brawny men chuckled as they lugged iron materials back and forth. They were probably older than Shuta's father, but they were all effortlessly handling metal poles as if they were mere twigs.

They were fixing up a small park in a residential area: tearing out the previous foundation, pouring fresh cement, and trimming back the overgrown trees. Shuta, now a member of the construction team, moved the WORK ZONE

AHEAD sign with some struggle. He was familiar with traffic cones, but had never touched one before, and had difficulty maneuvering the wheelbarrow full of gravel. And when he raked up the cut branches and leaves, he tripped over his own feet and fell, exasperating everyone.

Finally, it was time for their lunch break, and the crew made a beeline for the nearest convenience store. Some brought out packed lunches. Shuta just plopped on the ground, exhausted. A shadow loomed over him. Glancing up, he saw Kōsuke Higuchi.

"Here," said Kōsuke, holding out a lunch box.

"You bought this for me?" Shuta accepted the convenience store bento with a weak smile.

Kōsuke sat down next to him. "The boss and Satsuki told me to take care of you. I mean, I pretty much found you myself."

"*Found* me?" Shuta scoffed.

He was sure Kōsuke was younger than him, maybe about twenty. When Shuta asked, he answered he was twenty-two.

"Well, I, myself, was found by our boss when I was in a bad spot a few years ago." Kōsuke laughed casually.

"When you say 'bad spot,' do you mean you were out of work and were short of money or something?" asked Shuta.

"Exactly. I was flat broke and on the verge of robbing a

convenience store. But the boss happened to find me, and he dragged me to the office and beat some sense into me. You're lucky the cat saved you from experiencing the same fate."

There were many things Shuta wanted to ask and many things he didn't, but he decided not to take things too far. *I'm going to have to work as hard as I can.* He planned to quickly settle his repair debt and start searching for a new, decent job.

They completed their job before sunset. When they returned to the office, the veteran workers went inside, while the junior workers were tasked with unloading the equipment. But Shuta was shaky with exhaustion, so Kōsuke did most of the work.

Shuta hadn't pushed his body this hard in quite some time. He knew he was going to wake up with sore muscles the next day. When he entered the office on unsteady legs, he found Satsuki, the accountant, handing cash to a day laborer.

I didn't know there were businesses that operated like this in this day and age, he thought.

"Hey, Kagawa. You should come and get your pay, too," she said.

"Am I being paid by the day as well?"

"That's right. You haven't properly resigned from your

former company yet, have you? Make sure to complete your exit paperwork with them as soon as possible. It'd be a real pain for us if you were to have an accident or something right now."

"I see," said Shuta as he accepted the envelope. He hadn't contacted anyone at the company after fleeing from the office yesterday. It hadn't even crossed his mind to. He knew he needed to return and complete the exit process, but he just didn't feel up to it.

"And your cat," Satsuki stated bluntly. The pet carrier was at her feet. Bee's haunches were visible through the mesh.

"Oh, um, I'm sorry for bringing a cat to the workplace," he said.

"It's fine. You can't leave a cat alone for too long, right? Some cats are sensitive like that. Right, Bee? You've been such a good girl."

When Satsuki peered into the carrier, the cat wiggled her rump as if in response.

"Has she been in the carrier all day?" asked Shuta.

"No way. She was sitting in that box until a moment ago."

Chewed-up cardboard boxes were dotted around the room. It seemed like Bee had a blast playing with them. There was a bag of cat food next to the carrier, but it wasn't the one Shuta had brought.

"Did you buy this for the cat?"

"If the boss finds out that I did, he'll blow his top again," she said. "It'll be a problem, so you should get going soon."

Jinnai had been on another job, so Shuta hadn't seen him all day. If he discovered that Shuta was still giving Bee the food he'd previously yelled at him for, he might actually lose it.

"I'm sorry," said Shuta.

It was embarrassing. He hadn't had time to buy new food, so he had brought the food the clinic had given him. In the first place, the fact that he had brought his cat to the workplace was absurd. But he had asked Jinnai and Satsuki for permission to do so, thinking there was nothing to lose, and although they'd grumbled, they'd reluctantly agreed. Still, he couldn't do this every day. *I should go return the cat now.* Even though the idea crossed his mind, he was too tired to even lift the carrier.

"Hey, are you okay? You're unsteady on your feet," said Satsuki.

"I'm okay. I'm going to head out before the boss—"

Just then, workers caked in dirt entered the office in a noisy commotion. Among them was their boss, Jinnai. Unlike yesterday, when he was dressed in a dark suit like a yakuza, he was wearing the same work clothes as everyone else.

"Oh, you're still here."

Shuta panicked. *I've been caught.*

Jinnai crouched down, opened the pet carrier, and pulled out the cat, supporting her hind legs with a practiced hand. She remained calm in his arms. Jinnai looked happy.

"Bee, I bought you a collar."

"Did you skip out of work to go shopping?" Satsuki laughed bitterly.

"Are you kidding? I went to the pet store during my break. I placed a super-rush order to have them make it. Look at this." Jinnai pulled out a yellow collar from a neat little bag. "What do you think? Isn't it cute? It has your name on it. It's gold and shiny like your eyes."

Indeed, attached to the soft leather collar was a gold tag with the cat's name engraved on it. Shuta felt mixed emotions thinking about how this fierce-looking man dressed in construction gear went to a pet store and rush-ordered a custom-engraved cat collar.

"Thank you very much for taking the trouble to do that, Mr. Jinnai."

Jinnai's expression when he turned to Shuta was

completely different from his look when addressing Bee. As soon as he turned back to the cat, he was smiling again.

"Bee, have you eaten yet? Do you want to eat with me?"

"I already fed her." Satsuki sniffed loudly.

"Oh yeah? You've been having all the fun, I see, while your husband was toiling away."

"What are you saying? How does your schedule have anything to do with Bee?"

The couple began quarreling, with the cat—draped peacefully in Jinnai's arms—sandwiched between them.

I want to go home, thought Shuta. As he listened to their exchange, he felt his whole body creak with fatigue. They had even gotten a personalized collar for the cat. Would he be billed for it at some point?

It was already too late to return the cat to the clinic today. When he asked the couple if they could take care of the cat tomorrow, Jinnai and Satsuki looked at each other.

"If you insist, I don't mind."

"Me neither. I don't mind."

At least Bee wasn't going to be lonely while she was at this office.

—·—

The alarm was going off, but it sounded far away. Something was wrong. Shuta tried to get up, but he couldn't move. It was as if his limbs had been bound. He heard a soft meow coming from near his feet. It seemed Bee was already awake and probably wanted to be fed.

"Uhhh . . . uhhh."

He could make noises and move his facial muscles, but he had no control over his body from the neck down. His eyes began to well up with tears. He'd struggled with his mental health, but his physical health had always been fine. Things had taken a bizarre turn since he'd visited that peculiar clinic. As he lay on his back in bed, wallowing in self-pity, he heard someone speaking outside his apartment.

"I really don't know about this. Please take responsibility for whatever might happen." It was the familiar voice of the superintendent.

A male voice replied, "Fine. The man who lives in this room is my brother-in-law." It was Jinnai.

The key turned in the lock, and the front door opened.

"I knew it, boss. He's still sleeping."

Jinnai and Kōsuke barged into the room.

Shuta could barely raise his head. "Help me," he whispered.

Bee meowed and gently rubbed against Jinnai's leg as he bent down to give her a friendly pat on the forehead.

"All right, all right. You were locked in, you poor thing,"

said Jinnai, turning to leave the room with the cat in his arms.

"Please help me, too," Shuta pleaded. "I can't move."

"What? Don't be a brat."

"Boss," said Kōsuke. He peered down at Shuta in bed and laughed. "Didn't I tell you that I also couldn't get out of bed after the first day because my muscles were sore?"

"Young people these days are so weak. You're too skinny. I'll treat you to barbecue next time. You need to put on more muscle."

Shuta didn't want to eat barbecue later on. He'd rather do something about his sore muscles right now. He shook his body in an effort to rise, but it was hopeless. He heard Jinnai tut at him.

"Hey, Kōsuke, I'll wait in the car. Get the kid out of bed." He left the room, Bee still splayed in his arms.

Kōsuke helped Shuta to his feet and Shuta somehow managed to get dressed.

"Thank you, Kōsuke."

"No worries. But you're so lucky. I once pretended not to be home, and the boss kicked down my door and dragged me to work. I wonder if having a cat makes that big of a difference. Maybe I should get a cat, too."

"That cat's not mine. I'm just taking care of her for now."

To reveal that he'd been prescribed a cat would only make things more complicated, so Shuta kept the thought to himself as he picked up the pet carrier.

"Oh, you don't need that anymore," said Kōsuke.

"But I'll have to put her in this when I bring her home. I can't carry her in my arms all the way."

"A fancy pet carrier was delivered to the office first thing this morning. Along with some kind of fluffy cushion."

"Oh . . . Isn't that going a bit far? If they adore cats that much, they ought to get their own."

He followed Kōsuke out of the room. He walked in a bowlegged stance.

"I heard they used to have one."

"Oh, I see. I wonder if their cat died."

"Maybe."

"If so, they should get a new cat."

Instead of spending money on a freeloading cat, it would be much better for the Jinnais to have their own. Whatever the case, for the time being, he still needed to take Bee to the office. If that would keep his boss from kicking down his door, so much the better.

"Our work today's going to be even tougher than yesterday's." Kōsuke grinned.

Shuta shuddered.

Shuta carried Bee to the office every morning in the pet carrier Jinnai had bought. The sturdy, multifunctional, and stylish carrier looked much more expensive than the briefcase Shuta had carried while working at the brokerage firm. As soon as Shuta left Bee with Satsuki, the female part-timers at the office would surround her.

"Ever since this cat joined us, work's been so much more fun. Let's keep her in the office, Satsuki," said one of the women.

"Yes, we should. She's so gentle and friendly, even the boss approves. Bee-Bee, you're so cute," said another.

Even when the staff fussed over her, Bee remained unfazed. Sometimes, she'd rub up against them in a friendly manner; other times, she perched atop a shelf and refused to come down.

It was clear that when Bee was around, Jinnai was in a good mood. It wasn't only Jinnai. Though she didn't show it, Satsuki was also quite the cat lover. The fluffy cat bed sat at Satsuki's feet, but Bee didn't sleep in it. Instead, she buried herself inside the cardboard boxes piled up against the office wall, with her backside facing out.

Feeling somewhat guilty, Shuta said to the cat, "Bee,

you'd be so much more comfortable on the bed instead of in that tattered box."

"No way," Satsuki said as she filled out a payment slip. "Cats only do what they like."

"But you went to the trouble of buying her such a nice bed."

"It's okay. This also has a heating pad. It'll get cold in a little while, and then she won't want to leave it."

The workday hadn't officially begun yet, so the part-time clerks were still chatting among themselves, but Satsuki was already working at her desk. She was demanding but diligent.

It had been a week since Shuta had started working for the construction company. After about three days, the soreness in his body had subsided, but he was still exhausted. However, the pay was generous, so he would eventually save up enough money for the car repairs. But Bee had been prescribed to him for only ten days. By the time the weather turned cold, she'd be long gone.

"Did you use to have a cat?" Shuta asked Satsuki.

"We did. He passed away five years ago, but he had a long life. He was nineteen when he died. Remarkable, isn't it?"

Shuta didn't know cats could live that long. *They must*

have taken good care of the cat, he thought. *Well, if they love cats that much . . .*

"Will you get another cat?"

"But you see, our little one has already passed away," Satsuki replied without taking her eyes off the invoice she was working on. Though her voice and expression didn't change, it was clear she didn't want Shuta to pry further.

Kōsuke and other employees arrived. Shuta was assigned the task of carrying the equipment that day. By the time evening came, he was utterly drained.

Ten days after Shuta fled the brokerage firm, Yuina Sakashita asked him to meet her at a coffee shop near the station. The pet carrier lay under the table as they faced each other.

"Me, hospitalized?" asked Shuta.

"Yes, that's what I heard," answered Yuina. Perhaps curious about Bee, who was visible through the mesh panels, Yuina kept glancing down at her feet. "A friend in HR told me that she heard from Emoto that you were hospitalized for some stomach issue."

"So I haven't been fired yet?" Shuta thought it was strange that he hadn't heard from the company at all when he still had things that belonged to them. He didn't know how to feel about the fact that he was still employed by the firm. "From how Emoto acted, I was sure I'd be fired that very day."

"About that—a manager at his level doesn't have the authority to fire people at will. And no matter how terribly our company treats its employees, they won't terminate someone on the spot without following the proper procedures. Employees have rights, too."

"That may be true, but . . ."

As someone who had been treated as incompetent on a daily basis, Shuta felt like he had no rights at all. On top of that, if he was still officially an employee of the firm, it would mean he'd been AWOL for a while. It would be no surprise if he got fired.

"I don't know why Emoto lied, but I'm sure he's waiting for me to quit, to begin the process myself."

"Hey, I think you shouldn't be too hasty," said Yuina. The intense expression in her eyes made Shuta's heart skip a beat. She sipped her coffee. "The receipts that you asked me to look into—as I guessed, none of them had any record of being issued officially. My boss caught me investigating, then went directly to Emoto to ask him about it. Emoto said it was a misunderstanding, snatched the list from my boss, and ran off."

"So that's why he had the list."

"But I made sure to keep a copy of it. The matter is out of my hands now and is being looked into by the higher-ups. But an employee of a financial institution issuing their own receipts? It could only mean one thing." Yuina looked up at him.

Shuta understood the meaning of her upward glance. The truth was, he'd understood it all from the beginning. He lowered his voice. "Embezzlement?"

"Probably. So that's why I said you shouldn't resign prematurely. If anyone's going to have to quit, it's him."

The matter was too absurd.

Yuina's gaze dropped back to her feet. "Are you going to take this cat to the vet or something?" she asked.

"Huh? No, this one—" Shuta winced as he recalled he had another problem. "Yeah, I'm taking her to a clinic. It's nothing serious, but just in case."

"How old is it? What's its name?"

"Bee. Eight years old. She's a girl."

"Bee. What a cute name. Bee! Bee!"

Bee ignored her.

Shuta headed to the Nakagyō Kokoro Clinic for the Soul. It was dark and gloomy and the weight of the pet carrier seemed to bear down on his heart.

As he was about to enter the building, Shuta spoke to Bee. "Hey, Bee, are you happy at that office? Are people treating you well?"

As expected, Bee ignored him. Bee was a cat who exhibited a noticeable contrast in demeanor between when she was feeling affectionate and when she was feeling unfriendly. When he woke up in the morning, she would nuzzle against his hand as if to beg him to feed her urgently. When he offered her his palm, she would bury her head in it. She felt soft and fluffy to the touch. When Bee closed her eyes, it looked like she was smiling. This in turn always coaxed a smile from Shuta. For a long time, he struggled to do something even that simple, but now, Bee brought a glow to his face every day. Before he could utter a word, she would gaze up at him with anticipation.

When Shuta entered the clinic, he noticed the unfriendly nurse, Chitose, sitting at the reception window. Before he could say anything, she glanced up at him and said, "Mr. Kagawa, please come in. The doctor is expecting you."

He entered the examination room, where the doctor was waiting.

"Hello, Mr. Kagawa. You look well today," the doctor chirped.

Shuta felt a bit self-conscious about how noticeable the

improvement was. It wasn't because of any treatment he'd received at this clinic. Thanks to the physical demands of his new job, he'd begun sleeping well every night, and his appetite had returned. He'd even gained some weight.

The doctor tapped on his keyboard and nodded in understanding.

"Everything seems to be progressing well, and there seem to be no issues. Now, please return the cat," he said. "If that's all, I have an appointment with another patient coming up soon."

"Wait a minute."

"Hmm? Is there something else you need?"

Shuta felt a rush of panic at being ushered out so quickly. He hadn't made up his mind yet. The pet carrier was still on his lap.

"Um . . . can I borrow this cat for a little longer?"

The doctor cocked his head. "Your condition has improved, so I don't think you need to continue taking your prescription."

"No, um . . ."

In his mind, Shuta saw the faces of Jinnai and Satsuki, gazing at Bee with mesmerized expressions.

"I'm feeling better for sure. And the new company I'm at isn't a bad place to work, but it's not the kind of place that can offer job security in the long run. If possible, I'd like to work for a bigger, more stable corporation. So I'd like to keep the cat for a little longer."

"Didn't you work for such a company?" asked the doctor brightly. "You said yourself, Mr. Kagawa, that you were employed by a major brokerage firm—the kind you see in commercials. You've worked at a big, stable corporation."

The doctor's smile caught Shuta off guard. Shuta realized he'd gone round and round, and he was back in the same place. It was as if he were wandering the grid of Kyoto streets and couldn't find the exit.

Without waiting for a response, the doctor smiled bitterly and said, "The kind of place that can offer job security in the long run . . . Well, I suppose it's fine for you to keep the cat. There seem to be no side effects. But you can only keep her for five more days, as she's scheduled to be euthanized at the pound."

"Euthanized?"

"Yes, once her adoption deadline passes, she'll be put down."

What?

The doctor gave another smile and continued in his friendly Kyoto dialect.

"This cat, along with its two siblings, was trapped in a

house for days after their elderly owner passed away, until a neighbor reported it. There were three of them, and they were named A, Bee, and Cee. Isn't that fun?"

Bee. What a cute name. Bee.

Bee had just been complimented on her name not too long ago.

In his mind's eye, Shuta could see Satsuki and the part-time office staff greeting him so joyously. Shuta felt something hot surge and fill his chest. It was so intense that he found it hard to breathe.

"But Bee is a therapy cat for this clinic, right? Why not keep her here instead of returning her to the pound? Honestly, she was instrumental in my healing process."

"We're not a shelter. Once cats complete their service, they'll be returned to their rightful place."

The doctor's thin smile showed no emotion. If anything, it was Shuta's emotions that were in turmoil. *Bee is right here on my lap now.*

"Isn't there anything else you can do to find her a new owner? You can contact old patients or list her for adoption. Maybe you could find someone interested in adopting her online. After all, Bee is such a cutie."

It was all so sudden. Shuta struggled to gather his thoughts. He knew he was in no position to criticize the doctor, recognized that his knowledge of animal welfare was pretty basic. Still, the doctor's calm demeanor infuriated him. He glanced down at the carrier in his arms.

"If we all work together, we might be able to find someone who wants to adopt her. We just need to try harder," said Shuta.

"If we tried harder, you say?" said the doctor.

"That's right." Shuta looked up and, just as he expected, saw the doctor smiling.

"But it's not just this cat," continued Dr. Nikké. "Pet stores and shelters are actively trying to find homes for cats. Even the pounds are doing what they can. Despite all this, there seems to be no end to the number of cats with nowhere to go. It's not about meeting the conditions. A cat will only be adopted if it's able to have an emotional connection with its potential owner."

Emotional connection? Shuta didn't quite understand what that meant. If it was the answer to finding Bee a home, though, he wanted to know how to make it happen.

"So, how do you have an emotional connection?" Shuta asked.

"You're here because you don't know the answer to that. Come on; don't look so upset. Don't worry. You'll be cured in your remaining time with the cat. You've got just five more days left, so make sure you finish it all up."

Five more days, and that's it.

He couldn't accept the brutal truth that awaited the cat that had once been rescued. How could a life that had been spared be taken away once more?

"What about Bee's siblings? Are they here, too?" he asked, trembling.

The curtains behind the doctor were drawn closed. Chitose always brought the pet carrier through there. He didn't know what went on behind them.

"Bee's siblings passed soon after they were admitted. They died of starvation. That's the harsh reality."

Urged by the look in the doctor's eyes, Shuta picked up Bee's carrier and left the examination room. He passed the reception window, and Chitose didn't even look up. "Take care of yourself," she said, sounding cold and curt, like an unfriendly cat.

Two, then three days passed and Shuta still didn't know what to do. He took Bee to the construction office every day. Each day, more things that didn't belong in an office, such as a laser pointer and an electric fish-shaped cushion, appeared. Each new item made Shuta's stomach sink. Today was the fourth day of the latest prescription. Tomorrow, he would have to return Bee to the clinic.

The doctor had told him flatly that he would return Bee

to her "rightful place." Did he mean he would send her back to the pound, knowing what her fate would be?

"Hey, kid!"

Shuta was startled by a loud voice. The team's most senior member, an older man with a dark tan, was staring at him. In his arms were bags of sand.

"Shouldn't you young folks be doing the heavy lifting, not leaving it to an old man? You thoughtless brat!"

"I'm sorry," Shuta said, rushing to help.

He was always getting yelled at for being absentminded. He was used to it by now. Today, he was especially distracted and had been reprimanded several times, eventually even receiving a smack on the head.

On their way back to the office, Kōsuke discreetly consoled Shuta in the van.

"Don't let them get to you. The old guys have short tempers."

"Thank you. But it sure seems tough to work in construction at that age."

"Well, it is what it is. In exchange, they don't have to use their brains. As long as their bodies are strong, they'll get by. Despite how our boss appears, he's a sympathetic guy. He won't throw someone off the team because they're getting older. Kagawa, you should stick around as long as you can. See, you got some nice color on you."

Kōsuke smiled and held out his arm next to Shuta's. Shuta blinked. While Kōsuke's arm was still darker than his, his once-pale skin had somehow developed a tan.

Stick around as long as I can? It had never occurred to him to do such a thing. He remained speechless, and Kōsuke chuckled.

"No, that's no good. You're a college graduate. I'm sure you don't want to work for a shabby construction company," said Kōsuke.

When they returned to the office, they found the office staff gathered around Satsuki. Bee was curled up in her lap.

"I'm so jealous of you, Satsuki. I wish she'd sit on my lap, too."

"She's sleeping so comfortably. She's so cute!"

"What are you talking about? My legs went numb a while ago, and they hurt. It's so annoying that I can't move. Bee, why don't you go sit somewhere else?"

Despite what she said, Satsuki looked smug. She worked efficiently even with Bee on her lap. Bee had grown fond of Shuta, but she had never tried to crawl into his lap. He couldn't help but feel a little envious.

The sound of cars pulling into the lot signaled the return of another work crew.

As soon as Jinnai came through the door, he walked up to Satsuki. "Oh, Bee. Look at you, being such a good girl."

Bee remained in Satsuki's lap, but she widened her eyes and perked up her ears as if surprised.

Jinnai kneeled beside her, grinning from ear to ear. "Aren't you so clever? Oh, yes, you are, you cutie-patootie."

Jinnai's baby talk elicited a burst of laughter from Kōsuke. Jinnai's expression immediately darkened.

"What are you guys doing? You're supposed to be cleaning the heavy machinery as soon as you return to the office."

"Yes, boss," said Kōsuke, and he rushed out of the room.

Shuta knew that if he dawdled, he might get caught in the cross fire, so he followed Kōsuke. They went to the parking lot and hosed down the tires of the excavators and trucks. They worked silently, but eventually, Kōsuke muttered to himself, "What a cutie-patootie."

"Stop it, Kōsuke!" Shuta's shoulders shook with mirth. He had been holding back his laughter. Kōsuke grinned wickedly.

"It should be illegal for anyone with a face like our boss's to speak that way. And what did he mean by 'being such a good girl'? She was just sitting on Satsuki's lap."

No, I can't laugh. Everyone in the office will hear, thought Shuta. But neither he nor Kōsuke could hold it in anymore, and they both exploded with laughter. It had been months since Shuta had laughed like that. No, years.

After changing out of his work clothes and getting his daily pay, Shuta left the office with his coworkers. It was already dark outside. Kyoto at night was pretty quiet, with fewer people and cars around. Only the main streets were bustling at this hour.

As Shuta made his way down the street, he looked at the pet carrier in his arms.

"You'll be fine, Bee. You can stay with me forever."

Maybe it was from all that laughing, but his body felt warm, and his spirits were high. How hadn't he seen the easy solution before? He could simply adopt Bee. He had everything he needed.

He remembered the sensation of Bee's head nestled in the palm of his hand. He wasn't going to back down even if that weird doctor didn't like it. This must be what it meant to have an emotional connection. He enjoyed being around Bee. Every day, he was soothed by her cuteness. She was sure to bring him happiness for a long time to come.

When his apartment block came into view, he stopped in his tracks. Under the dim streetlamp stood Emoto. He seemed to have already noticed Shuta approaching and was smiling faintly.

"Mr. Emoto . . ."

"Kagawa! Don't you look well!"

Emoto's usual demeanor was replaced with a humble smile and a casual tone.

Shuta stood frozen. Emoto approached him and placed his hand on Shuta's shoulder.

"I was worried about you because you ran out so suddenly. But it's all right. I've been covering for you," he said with a forced laugh. He then lowered his voice, seemingly worried about being overheard. "So, Kagawa. I'm not sure what to say. It looks like you got me all wrong, so I figured I needed to set things straight. It was Kijima who was doing some pretty crazy stuff with my clients."

"Mr. Emoto, I'm no longer involved in this matter . . ."

"No, listen to me. I thought it was strange that Kijima suddenly stopped showing up at work. It turns out that he's been collecting money directly from elderly customers, claiming he had profitable opportunities for them. Obviously, he didn't tell the company. Had me fooled, too. I even sent him to my clients to boost his numbers, so I feel responsible for this."

"Mr. Emoto . . ."

Shuta remembered Kijima's expression as he mentioned his excitement about seeing the elderly customer he'd befriended. Emoto's obvious lies and excuses made Shuta's heart ache. Despite his intense dislike for the man, he found himself feeling sorry for him.

"Even so, there's nothing I can do about it. I plan on quitting," said Shuta.

"What are you talking about, Kagawa? We're both victims, aren't we? It was Kijima. He did everything on his own. You tell the company this, okay?" As Emoto's voice grew fiercer, he drew closer to Shuta.

Shuta's back was against the wall of the apartment building. "Please calm down."

"Calm down? You have it easy. All you have to do is quit, but my whole life is at stake here!" Emoto's words echoed through the dark streets.

Bee began to yowl and rattle the carrier violently, as if she were screaming. Shuta clutched the carrier to his chest with both hands.

"Bee. It's okay. Relax."

Emoto clasped his hands together in supplication. "Please, Kagawa. I have a family. What if I get sued? I just need you to align your story with mine for a little while. In the meantime, I'll return all the money I collected to my clients."

Shuta shook his head.

"If you tell the company the truth, they might forgive you. I also plan to tell them everything I know." Shuta tried not to drop the carrier in which Bee was rampaging.

Emoto's face turned blank. Then he let out a weak laugh. "Tell them the truth? You self-important little—"

"Mr. Emoto—"

"No, you're right." Underneath Bee's relentless caterwauling, Emoto sounded strangely calm. He turned his shadowy eyes toward the carrier. "Have you got a cat in there? I didn't know you had a cat."

"Um, well, yes," said Shuta. He felt a chill go down his spine. His grip around the carrier tightened, but Bee didn't stop crying.

Emoto broke into a grin, then looked up at Shuta's apartment building. "You live here, don't you? A building like this doesn't typically allow pets. You must be keeping your cat in secret. Isn't that a bit dishonest?"

Shuta's jaw dropped. Emoto rubbed his chin in triumph.

"I'm going to call your building's management company first thing tomorrow. You, too, should just *tell the truth*. Tell them the whole truth. Hey, am I the only bad person here? Embezzling money is bad, but secretly keeping a cat is okay? You're being deceitful, too. Don't act like you're the only honest one."

Emoto laughed, but he also looked on the verge of tears.

Clutching the pet carrier more tightly than ever, Shuta

fled. The laughter behind him gradually faded into the distance.

Relieved to see that the lights in the office were still on, Shuta made his way inside to find Jinnai and Satsuki. Satsuki looked concerned.

"What's wrong, Kagawa?"

"Here . . . the cat . . ."

Out of breath from running so fast, he collapsed onto the floor and pointed to the pet carrier.

Satsuki took it with a confused look. "What happened? You're drenched in sweat."

"Please take in the cat. Make Bee yours," pleaded Shuta. His gaze met Bee's, her golden eyes fixed on him through the carrier's mesh panel. His own eyes began to well up.

Standing over Shuta, Jinnai looked stern. "What do you mean? Give me a proper explanation."

"Bee is not my cat. She's from the pound. Tomorrow's the end of her adoption period; after that, she'll be put down."

"Put down?" Satsuki squeaked.

Jinnai remained silent.

"I thought I'd just adopt Bee, that it would work. But then, my department head—no, my apartment management—

found out about her, and I can't keep her anymore. Will you please take Bee in? You both love cats. Bee adores you. Please."

Shuta got onto his knees and bowed deeply, his forehead touching the floor. When he looked up a few moments later, he saw Jinnai's lips were set in a tight line, and Satsuki was looking baffled.

"Honey—" said Satsuki, addressing her husband.

"No. We cannot take the cat." Jinnai's voice was deep and bitter.

Shuta shook. "Why not?"

"We've decided not to have cats anymore. After our cat died, we swore never to get another one ever again. I cannot break that vow, no matter what."

"Boss."

Jinnai dropped to one knee and leveled a penetrating stare.

"Listen. You said you wanted to keep Bee, didn't you? Didn't you?"

"Yes, I did. But—"

"Then you have to be responsible for her until the end. If you can't keep her, then you should do everything possible to change things so that you can. Is there anything else you can do?"

You can stay with me forever. Shuta looked through the

mesh at Bee, then clasped his hands together. There, he felt something soft and warm—a fluffy tennis ball. The cat had become his without his knowing, and she was never going to leave him. Just as Jinnai and Satsuki held the memory of their late cat close to their hearts, Shuta knew he would forever carry this warmth within his heart.

The golden eyes peering at Shuta through the small window were not worried about a thing. At least they didn't seem to be worried. It was no longer a trivial matter of whether it was fun to live with a cat, or whether she was cute. He might be evicted from his apartment. His job was unstable, and he had little money saved up. What could he do?

Shuta rested his forehead on the floor again. "Please let me work permanently for you, boss! Please let me stick around even after I finish paying back the car repair bill! I'll move out of my place tomorrow. I will find an apartment that allows cats, and I will keep Bee. So, can you please continue to look after Bee here while I'm working? I promise to work even harder."

He wasn't going to raise his head from the floor until he got an okay from Jinnai.

He heard Jinnai snort.

"You need to move."

"What?" Shuta lifted his head. "Yes. I'm going to a real estate agency tomorrow."

"What an idiot. You think you can find a pet-friendly place that quickly? I'll talk to a real estate agent I know, but for now, take your stuff and move into the room above this office. If it's just for a little while, I can care for Bee. Hey, Bee. Do you want to snuggle with me today?"

Jinnai took hold of the pet carrier, flopped down on the leather sofa, and threw his legs up on the table. His manner was brusque, but his face betrayed his delight.

A little stunned, Shuta savored the feeling of finally putting down roots somewhere.

Satsuki gave a wry smile. "That's why I said you need to settle your affairs with your old company. And find a new apartment quickly. Otherwise, the old man won't come into work until you do."

"Absolutely." Shuta stifled his laughter.

Fate works in mysterious ways. Not long ago, he'd been aimlessly wandering the streets of Nakagyō, and now here he was. He was going to be busy from now on. First, he had to go back to that clinic and inquire about keeping Bee.

What would that strange doctor say?

When Shuta reached out to Yuina to let her know he'd decided to resign officially, she responded immediately.

"Emoto hasn't been in the office lately. He's been suspended pending the outcome of the investigation."

They were walking south along Tominokoji Street. Shuta had gone to the brokerage firm first thing that day, completed the exit paperwork, and knocked out what he could in one day. When he told Yuina about the situation with Bee, she offered to accompany him to the clinic.

"Suspension, huh? I hope he'll tell the truth."

Shuta held the pet carrier firmly in his hand. Bee seemed calm today.

"You got the worst of it in the end. You didn't have to quit," said Yuina.

"If I didn't quit now, I'd have left eventually."

"Well, the company treats its employees like dirt," said Yuina. She had a conflicted look on her face. "I'll do my best to make things a little better. I like my job now, so I'm not going to complain—I'll take action. If we give it our all, we can change things."

"Yes, we can change things."

Shuta had a preconceived notion that Jinnai's company—and the construction industry in general—was corrupt. But he found the job surprisingly suited his nature and he didn't dislike it.

After crossing a few intersections, Yuina stopped.

"So, where is this amazing clinic? Haven't we been going round in circles for a while?"

Shuta, who had confidently taken the lead, seemed lost again. Yuina was beginning to be fed up.

"What's the name of the district?" she asked.

"Well, it doesn't have a district name. The address is made up of street names in that unique Kyoto style. It's confusing—east of Takoyakushi Street, south of Tominokoji Street, west of Rokkaku Street, north of Fuyacho Street, Nakagyō Ward, Kyoto."

"What kind of address is that? Go east, south, west, then north? Aren't we just going around the block?"

"Right. I guess."

Still, he had been to the clinic before. If they walked around the neighborhood for a bit, they should come upon that dark alley. But today, neither the alley nor the building was anywhere in sight. No matter how many times they circled the area, they could not find it. They stood together in the middle of the street. Bee began to meow and shift uncomfortably in her carrier. "Maybe she's hungry."

Yuina looked up and down the street they had just walked through. "The clinic isn't here."

"You're right."

But the clinic was no dream or illusion. The weight of

the cat in his hand was very real. Yet he could no longer get to the clinic. Once you had entered the grid of streets, whether the clinic existed or not depended on the moment. Such unique randomness was characteristic of the streets of Kyoto.

Shuta looked at Yuina. She was laughing, her head tilted quizzically to one side. Shuta laughed, too. The two of them began walking down the street without turning back.

Margot

2

Margot

"Man, this is pretty shabby," muttered Koga testily.

The building was located at the end of a dank alley, sandwiched between two equally decrepit-looking structures. From the main road, the alley looked like nothing more than a gap between two buildings. The structure itself was gloomy. The sky above was clear, but darkness shadowed his every step. It mirrored his current emotional state.

Standing in the entrance, Koga peered down the long and narrow corridor.

"Good grief. Why am I even here?" he mumbled as he walked down the hallway toward the stairs. Climbing up to the second and then the third floor, he found himself running out of breath. "Why the hell do I have to visit a goddamn shrink or 'mental health professional' or whatever? Mental health, my ass."

There was nothing to like about this situation. By the time he reached the fifth floor, he was wheezing, his shoulders heaving up and down.

"What's with this strange address anyway? What a mess."

East of Takoyakushi Street, south of Tominokoji Street, west of Rokkaku Street, north of Fuyacho Street, Nakagyō Ward, Kyoto.

These kinds of addresses, which provided the intersections in all four directions, were intended to make navigating the chessboard-like streets of Kyoto easier. But the directions he was given to the clinic were a mess, likely to have been passed down by people unfamiliar with the city. He had overheard a conversation in which someone recommended Nakagyō Kokoro Clinic for the Soul. He had never been that keen to visit the clinic in the first place, and even now, as he stood in front of the clinic's door, he was hesitating.

Maybe I shouldn't do this. Wait, no—I got off my butt to come all the way here. I might as well get a checkup, even if it's just for my own peace of mind.

But stepping into a mental health clinic, no matter how informally, was no simple undertaking for Koga, a man in his fifties who came from a generation that harbored deep skepticism toward psychiatry.

I should go home. Wait, no—I took today off to come here . . .

As Koga stood there debating with himself, a man appeared at the end of the hallway. He strode past Koga and headed for the unit adjacent to the clinic. As he slowly opened the door, he cast Koga a wary glance.

Worried he might look suspicious, Koga hastily pushed open the door to the Nakagyō Kokoro Clinic for the Soul. Despite being old and heavy, the door glided open, revealing an unexpectedly pristine interior. The small, tidy reception window was unattended. He had rushed up the stairs yet found himself suddenly lacking the courage to let anyone know he was there. *Should I just turn around now?* As he stood in the doorway and dithered over what to do next, he heard the pattering of footsteps, and soon, a nurse appeared.

"Hello. You're a new patient, right? Please come in."

"Well, I'm not—"

"Please come in."

Without so much as a glance in Koga's direction, the nurse, who looked to be in her late twenties, motioned for him to enter. Koga felt he had no choice but to do as told.

He spotted a small sofa in the waiting room, but when he was about to take a seat, the nurse snapped at him. "The waiting room is for patients with appointments. The doctor is available to see you now, so please make your way toward the back." There was something both gentle and sharp about her distinct Kyoto accent.

Koga was miffed. *What a disagreeable woman.* She reminded him of the very person responsible for his anxieties. He scowled at her, but he could see she wasn't paying him any attention.

Pouting in frustration, he walked into the examination room. It was a compact space, furnished with only a desk with a computer and two simple chairs. Privacy curtains hung at the back of the room. He wondered about the layout of the place, which seemed quite basic for a medical facility.

Koga's doubts grew when the curtains flew open and a doctor in a white coat appeared, a slender man of about thirty. He was considerably younger than Koga and had the kind of delicate facial features he knew his daughter, Emiri, would find appealing. *Is a kid like him qualified to practice psychiatric medicine?* Koga, who often received pointed remarks about his protruding belly and old-man vibes from his wife, couldn't help but feel a bit resentful.

"Hello. I see you're new to our clinic," said the doctor.

His inflection, thick with the Kyoto dialect, made him sound like a more mature town doctor.

"Well, I suppose, yes."

"Out of curiosity, how did you find out about us?"

"A friend of a friend . . . no one in particular," mumbled Koga. He couldn't recall the exact source of the information, but he had been desperately eavesdropping on a conversation when someone mentioned a good psychiatric clinic.

The doctor let out a peculiarly cheerful chuckle. "I see," he said. "Well, that's a problem. From time to time, patients do drop in like this, having heard about us from someone. But as you can see, there are only two of us here, the nurse and me, so we're not accepting any new patients."

"Wait. What?" Having been skeptical about the clinic until a moment ago, Koga suddenly felt a rush of anxiety as it seemed he might be turned away. "I took half a day off from work to come here. Isn't this a mental health psychiatric clinic or whatever? I have issues and need an examination."

"Mental health? Psychiatry?" The doctor cocked his head in puzzlement. "Ha! That sounds cool." He dissolved into more chuckles. Koga looked at him blankly. "Well, since you came all the way here, I'll make a special exception for you. Now, tell me your name and age."

"I-I'm Yusaku Koga. I turn fifty-two next month."

"What brings you in today?"

He's been a bit uppity, but I guess he's agreed to see me. Koga scowled. *Even if I share my feelings, no one will understand what I'm going through. Not the doctor, not my family, not my coworkers. I'm an outcast.*

He wrung his hands in his lap and dropped his gaze.

"I have a work-related problem. I find it challenging to get along with a new employee who joined our office about three months ago. A—what d'you call it—diversity, equity, and inclusion hire or whatever. A female supervisor. And she . . . How can I describe her? She's extremely bubbly, and I find her displeasing."

That's right. Hinako Nakajima. I just don't like her.

Hinako was forty-five years old and he considered her too old to be always so cheerful. Perhaps it was because she was single, but everything about her was loud: her outfits, her voice, her gestures. And she was always laughing. Just remembering her laughter made Koga nauseous.

"I work for an outsourced call center, and almost all our staff, except me, is female. So the workplace is a lonely place for me. But that's not a big deal. I've done a reasonably good job listening to the complaints of both my coworkers and any chronic complainer customers. But since that woman joined our office, the atmosphere has totally changed. I don't know why, but I find her voice incredibly grating."

The call center covered a lot of floor space, and it had numerous workstations equipped with phones, on which operators spoke directly to customers. Dealing with a wide variety of callers and their issues placed a lot of stress on the staff.

As a middle manager, Koga's job was to oversee the operation. And on occasion, he had to jump on calls himself to offer profuse apologies. Although he'd worked at the same company for fifteen years, he was still only a section manager. He'd been yelled at by customers, but he'd never gotten into trouble at work. His days were monotonous, but they were mostly tranquil. The call center's general manager was a man with even less potential for career advancement than Koga, and he was a year away from retirement. Everyone had assumed that Koga would take his place.

And yet . . .

Out of the blue, Hinako Nakajima had turned up at their office from Tokyo. She was appointed to a newly created role of deputy general manager, making her Koga's new boss all of a sudden.

"I like it, I like it, I like it!" Koga clenched his fists in his lap. "I can't get those words out of my head. They keep ringing in my ears, especially in the middle of the night.

When I'm trying to sleep, I hear, 'I like it, I like it, I like it!' like an incantation."

Koga relaxed his fists and looked up. *What?* He had just bared his soul, but the young doctor was looking blankly away from him and picking his nose.

"What are you looking at, doctor? Did you hear what I just said?"

"Hmm? Oh, of course I did. Yes, yes, you work at a call center. Seems stressful. So, what's the matter?"

The doctor's flippant tone made Koga lose his temper.

"I can't sleep! That woman's voice haunts my dreams. I haven't slept properly in weeks! I find myself zoning out at work more and more. If this carries on, I'm going to lose my mind."

Koga's face was scarlet, and his breath was ragged from his outburst. The doctor remained unperturbed, detached.

"I see. It's tough, not being able to sleep." The doctor turned to his desk and began tapping away on his computer keyboard. "We'll prescribe you a cat, and let's monitor how you feel for a while. Oh, you're in luck. We just got back a particularly effective cat." He spun around in his chair, turning his back to Koga.

"Chitose, can you bring me the cat?"

"Yes," came the answer, and the nurse from earlier came into the room. In one arm was a cat with a black and reddish-brown coat. In the other arm was a pet carrier, which she placed on the desk. Then she handed the cat to the doctor.

The doctor took the cat in his arms and began giving it long strokes from head to tail.

"This is a highly effective cat," he said. "It's already booked for another patient after you, so I can only give you a ten-day prescription. But that should be enough. Here you go."

The doctor thrust the cat at Koga. Koga was so startled that he instinctively slid his chair back. But there was nowhere to go in the small room. He was forced to accept the cat in his arms.

"Hey, hey, hey. What is this?"

"A cat. Works really well for insomnia," said the doctor. "Here, I'll write you a prescription, so please take it to reception. Now, take care."

"Is this a joke? Treat my insomnia with a cat? What's that going to do? It's not worth a fart in a windstorm!"

"Please don't fart. Even cats can't stand bad odors. Don't worry. Cats can solve most problems. Oh, and if you see a patient in the waiting room, will you tell them to come in?"

The doctor handed Koga a small piece of paper and pressed the pet carrier into his hands.

Koga fled the room as if chased. There was no one in the waiting room. At the reception window, the nurse gave him a paper bag. With some effort, Koga managed to push the cat into the carrier. He had interacted with the creature only briefly, but his clothes were already covered in hair.

Insomnia after the age of fifty. An outcast at work and at home. He was responsible for looking out for his team's mental health, yet he was concealing his own struggles. With the intention to address all that, he had visited the clinic in secret, and now he found himself peering down at his cat fur–covered self.

"What in heaven's name?" he muttered.

Koga's home was located along a major train line, a short distance from Kyoto City. His house was a twenty-minute walk from the station. The house came with a garage that could barely accommodate one car, and he still had fifteen years left on his mortgage. Still, he considered himself the king of his castle. His wife was a homemaker. His only daughter was in college. The addition of a cat to the household was nothing to him.

And yet, he couldn't help glancing around cautiously as he entered his house.

"I'm home," he called softly as the hum of the television

in the living room reached his ears. His wife, Natsue, was likely lounging on the sofa.

He looked at the pet carrier in his arms and felt at a loss. While he had grumbled internally the entire time since he'd left the clinic, he had now brought the cat all the way home. Having no experience caring for animals, he knew he would need his family's cooperation.

How do I explain this to them? I have trouble sleeping—so I was prescribed a cat? Apparently, cats can solve most problems?

While he was debating what to say, Natsue emerged from the living room.

"Home already?"

"Uh, yeah." Koga hid the large carrier behind him.

"You need to let me know if you're coming home early. I haven't started the rice cooker yet."

"I'm sorry. There's no need to rush to make dinner."

He had already managed to put Natsue in a bad mood. To get his daughter on his side seemed like the smart move now.

"Where's Emiri?" he asked. "As I'm home early, maybe we'll eat dinner together for a change."

"What are you talking about? Emiri left yesterday for that overnight trip with her friends from some college club. I've mentioned this to you quite a few times already."

"Oh, really?"

"Seriously, you never listen to anything I say."

Natsue let out a sigh, unable to conceal her displeasure. Not wanting to upset her further, Koga attempted to sneak his bags upstairs, but he was immediately caught.

"What's in that big bag?" asked Natsue. "You didn't buy more plastic model kits, did you? I told you we don't have room for them anymore!"

"No, I didn't. I got this from the company. It's not anything impor—"

Natsue let out a string of explosive sneezes. Startled by the unexpected outburst, the cat caused the pet carrier to rattle and shake.

"Hey, behave!" hissed Koga.

"Wait, don't tell me." Natsue looked into the case and sneezed again. "No! It's a cat!"

"Yes. So, today, I went to a clinic—"

"Stay away from me! I'm allergic to cats!" Natsue covered her nose with the sleeve of her dress and glared at him with tearful eyes.

Koga was bemused. "Allergic? Since when?"

"Since before we got married! I've told you many times!"

She rushed out of the room.

Koga stood stunned. He had no choice but to lug the

pet carrier and the paper bag upstairs to the spare room they were using as storage. He set the carrier on the floor and sat next to it.

"Allergies, huh? Oh, boy," he muttered. "She was sneezing a lot, so maybe she *is* actually allergic to cats."

His eyes met those of the cat peeking through the mesh panel of the carrier. It stared at him as if waiting to see what he might do.

"What? Don't look at me like that. I've got this under control. I'm the head of this household. I'll take care of this. Just sit tight. Please."

When he went back downstairs, Natsue was waiting for him in the living room with narrowed eyes. The look on her face made it clear things were not going to go smoothly.

"So, you know, that cat was actually prescribed to me at one of those mental health clinics or whatever. The doctor said that cats can solve most problems—"

"Are you kidding me?" Natsue was furious. "You're not seriously planning to keep this cat without consulting me, are you?"

"No, no, no. I'm just looking after it for a bit. I'm returning the cat to the clinic after ten days. Just ten days. I'll take responsibility for its care during this time."

After several minutes of Koga's desperate efforts to appease her, Natsue gave in.

"Please don't let the cat roam around the house. Keep it out of the living room and the bedroom. It's the hair that bothers me. Whenever I touch a cat, my nose gets all itchy—" Natsue sneezed again. "Look, you're covered in cat hair. Go outside and shake off your clothes!"

"Okay, okay."

When Koga went outside to brush down his clothes, he spotted the neighbors watching him curiously. He wondered why he, the king of his castle, was being subjected to this. Maybe it was time he showed them a thing or two. But he could feel fury radiating from Natsue, who was in the kitchen preparing dinner. This was not the moment for him to voice his grievances.

He dragged himself back upstairs to the spare room and snapped open the door of the pet carrier. The cat remained tucked away inside. The paper bag contained all the essentials for taking care of the cat, such as food, a water bowl, and kitty litter. Koga sat cross-legged on the tatami floor and read the instruction leaflet.

> NAME: Margot. Female. Estimated to be 3 years old. Mixed breed. Feed moderate amounts of cat food in the morning and at night. Water bowl must always be full. Clean

> kitty litter as needed. Generally independent and can be left alone. When the cat is asleep, make sure to close the door to her room. If she seems unhappy about being shut in, open all the doors in the house and let her come and go as she pleases. That's all.

The instructions were simple. Regardless of whether the cat preferred the door open or closed, he couldn't have the cat wandering around Natsue, so he'd have no choice but to keep the door of their room closed that night. Otherwise, it seemed like he could leave the cat be.

He went to the bathroom to fill up a bowl with water and the other with dry food and placed both in the corner of the room.

"What else?"

While he was looking up feline care tips on his phone, the cat peeked around the edge of the carrier. She emerged slowly, then took a restless look around the room.

Margot was a quintessential mixed-breed cat, her coat a mixture of black and reddish-brown. She also had a couple of white patches at the tips of her paws and at the base of her neck. She wasn't classically beautiful, but she exuded an aura of strength. Her eyes were the color of green tea, with a black vertical line in the center. The sharp upward tilt of her eyes lent her a touch of wildness. Her lean, long-limbed frame brought to mind the muscularity of a light-weight boxer.

"What's up with you? You look so strong for a female cat. It says you're mixed breed, but isn't there a name for cats that look like you?"

A search online revealed that she was most likely considered a tortoiseshell cat. They were known to be intelligent, alert, and affectionate.

He noticed that the cat had come to sit beside him and was staring at him with piercing tea-green eyes.

"What is it? You're scaring me. Margot, right? Listen, Margot. I'm the master of the house. I call the shots here, so don't you even think about scratching me."

Margot's eyes showed no emotion. She tilted her head a little, and then, to his relief, she moved toward the corner of the room and began to chomp. Online sources cautioned that if a cat refused to eat for three days, it should be taken to a veterinarian.

"Well, that's to be expected. Her role requires her to stay with different people, so no wonder she's well-trained. But what a strange idea. A cat that helps with sleep."

With her back to him, the cat crunched away at her meal. Her long tail swayed from side to side. It seemed to have a hypnotic effect on him; owing to his recent months of sleep deprivation, he felt his eyelids grow heavy.

Meow, meow, meow.

Meow, meow, meow.

Plugging his ears or pressing his pillow over his head was useless. Unable to stand it any longer, he threw off his blanket. How many times had he gotten up already?

In the darkness, Margot continued meowing at the small window. Not being allowed to take Margot into the bedroom due to Natsue's allergies but reluctant to put the cat he had been prescribed to treat his insomnia in a separate room, Koga decided to bring a full set of bedding into the spare room to sleep there with the cat.

At first, Margot had been quiet. With her tiny paws, she'd kneaded the corner of the cushion he had set out for her as if she were giving it a massage. Her adorable gestures made even Koga, who was over fifty, feel a heartwarming rush. It somehow reminded him of his daughter's early childhood.

After a while, however, Margot's incessant cries began to trouble him. She did not stop whimpering. Concerned something might be wrong with her, he searched for answers on his phone. He read that if a cat's living environment wasn't properly set up, it might meow throughout the night due to stress. Having been suddenly placed in an unfamiliar home, Margot was struggling to sleep.

At first, Koga felt sorry for her, but after two, then three hours, he could no longer endure it.

Meow, meow, meow. She kept crying toward the window.

"Hey, cut it out. I have work tomorrow," he said.

Despite his insomnia, on an average night he would grow drowsy and manage to doze off after a few hours. Strangely, by the time the sky started to brighten, he'd be sound asleep, only to be roused by his alarm clock. His sleep was brief, but it wasn't completely nonexistent.

Tonight was different. Sleep eluded him entirely. Normally, Hinako Nakajima would appear in his dreams and shower him with compliments, but instead, Margot's constant cries kept him up.

"Hey, be quiet, will you? Why won't you sleep? Are you cold, sleeping on that cushion?" In the darkness, he reached for his robe and threw it over Margot. But her cries didn't stop. He pulled his blanket over his head.

I need to sleep. I need to sleep.

Meow, meow, meow.

I need to sleep. Even if just for a little while, or my body won't hold up.

Meow, meow, meow.

Before Koga knew it, light was streaming in through the window. By then, Margot was finally curled up inside the robe, her eyes closed. Even when the alarm clock rang, she pretended not to hear it. He, on the other hand, hadn't slept a single second. His eyes were bloodshot, his hair was a mess, and his stomach churned with nausea.

As he groaned and retched in the bathroom, Natsue frowned. "What are you going to do about that cat?" she asked. "I won't be able to care for it. I can't even touch it."

Koga groaned again. "I've put out food and water, and I've cleaned the litter box, so don't worry about her. I'll take care of the rest when I get back home."

"But is it okay to lock a cat in a room? Isn't it cruel?" she asked.

If you think so, just leave all the doors in the house open for her. His mind was in a haze, and he wasn't even sure if he had said that out loud. Koga went about his morning routine in a daze. *"A highly effective cat," my foot. That quack doctor.*

As always, when he arrived at the call center, Hinako Nakajima was already there.

"Good morning, Mr. Koga!" Her cheerful voice reverberated in Koga's sleep-deprived head. "Your tie! I like it! It gives you a youthful look!"

Before he could respond, Hinako was already greeting other employees. "Good morning! Oh, did you trim your bangs? I like it! You look great. Good morning! Well, those shoes—I like them! Good morning! Thank you for working late yesterday. The report was perfect. I like how driven you are!"

"How many more compliments is she going to give?" Koga muttered at his desk. He hadn't slept a wink last night, but Hinako's incessant *I like its* hadn't haunted his dreams either.

Hinako had been like this ever since she had joined their office. Regardless of whether someone was a superior or a subordinate, she showered them with praise for every little thing. From people's appearance to job performance, even the contents of a convenience store bento or the canned juice they were drinking—all were subjects of her unwavering admiration.

"She's so high-spirited every day. It's exhausting for everyone around her," murmured Fukuda, the call center's general manager, who sat opposite Koga. Koga pegged him as an unambitious, nonconfrontational type who likely shared his low opinion of Hinako. Fukuda, too, was a man who struggled with changes in his environment.

"I don't get why the Tokyo head office thrust someone like her onto us. They say this and that about our high staff turnover rate, but it's always the same no matter who's in charge. Quitters gonna quit."

Koga responded with a noncommittal "Huh." Normally, he would have smirked, but perhaps because he was sleepy, he couldn't muster the enthusiasm to side with Fukuda today.

Hinako was still energetically greeting team members as they arrived.

"Well, she'll be gone sooner or later. I don't care if they're looking to 'reform' or 'renew' our team—if she doesn't deliver, Head Office will have to reconsider her role. Anyway, I hope things don't change too much."

Not wanting to engage with the cheerless Fukuda, Koga remained silent. He neither liked nor disliked Fukuda. But Hinako had come to Kyoto from Tokyo on her own to become Fukuda's deputy. Even a cat can't sleep soundly in an unfamiliar house. Surely, Hinako was putting in her fair share of effort. Wasn't there a way to be more supportive?

Then it struck him: much like Fukuda, he hadn't been supportive.

"'I like it,' is it?"

Despite his tottering, sleep-deprived state, Koga managed to get through his tasks. When lunchtime arrived, as usual, he ate alone in a corner of the cafeteria, while Hinako sat surrounded by a large group of women.

"Check this out, Hinako. This is from my kid's field day." The coworker showed Hinako her phone.

Hinako widened her eyes dramatically in response. "Oh, that's Rina, right? She's in second grade, isn't she? Look at her run!"

"Hinako, take a look at this video from my child's piano recital."

"Izumi's so talented! And her dress is so lovely! A career as a professional pianist could be on the horizon."

Hinako reacted to every single video and photo shown to her. It was always boisterous around Hinako. Koga had never seen the staff so animated.

"I like it . . . Like it, like it, like it."

Sleep. Sleep. Sleep. Meow, meow, meow.

Before he knew it, he was dozing with his eyes open. At the adjacent table, two of the younger women were giggling over something on their phones.

"Look, isn't this great?"

"Really nice. That's definitely going to make the boyfriend happy, don't you think?"

More giggles.

Meow, meow, meow.

His eyelids felt incredibly heavy, as if his eyes were about to roll back. He wasn't going to lose to her. Even he could spout out an "I like it" and praise people like Hinako. With unsteady feet, he approached the two women.

"That's nice. I like it!"

The two women jerked their heads up. On one phone was an image of a bright red lace bra-and-panties set.

". . . So nice—the weather today is so nice."

Pretending to look into the distance, Koga walked away. He broke into a cold sweat. He was too scared to look back, imagining what they might be saying about him.

I like it. I like it. Damn it. What's there to like? Am I an idiot?

Koga bit his lip. He shouldn't have imitated Hinako. His head was foggy from sleep deprivation. Tonight, he was going to lock that cat in another room.

When he returned home feeling queasy, he was greeted by joyful laughter. Natsue and Emiri were in the living room.

"I'm back," he said softly, but neither of them turned around. He craned his neck to see what they found so amusing. There was Margot, lying on the rug.

"Oh, you're home." Natsue glanced briefly at him and then turned her attention back to Margot.

"You're so cute, Margot. You're such a well-behaved girl."

Natsue was stroking Margot's outstretched body. Margot looked grumpy but allowed it to happen. Natsue wasn't sneezing, and her eyes weren't red.

"Is it okay for you to be touching the cat? What happened to your allergy?"

"I didn't have a choice but to go to the hospital. But my allergies aren't that severe. They gave me eye drops and some mild medication. They also recommended brushing her regularly to prevent excessive shedding and keeping her litter box clean. Poor little Margot, cooped up all day in that room. What a terrible daddy you have."

"Wait, you're the one who said she shouldn't roam around the house."

Koga noticed the instruction leaflet lying on the table. The food and water dishes had also been moved to the living room.

"Hey, Dad, are we keeping this kitty?"

Koga was taken aback by Emiri's smile. When was the last time he'd seen his daughter smile like this? Since she started college, or perhaps even high school, their interactions had been limited to the occasional conversation, and it had been a while since she had smiled at him like that.

"N-no, we're just taking care of her temporarily. We have to return her in a few days."

"Really? I wish she could stay with us forever. She's so cute and silky."

Emiri ran her hand down Margot's body. Margot appeared miffed, but she remained docile.

"Mom, let's get a cat. I promise to take care of it."

"What are you talking about? You're busy with classes and extracurriculars. I'll end up having to take care of her."

"That's not true. I'll take care of her. Right, Margot?"

With both hands under her front legs, Emiri lifted Margot up. Her body stretched a surprising amount.

"Look, Mom. How funny! Look how long she gets."

"That's amazing!"

The two were excited, but Koga wasn't much amused. *It's the same as always. I'm always left out—at work and at home.*

Holding Margot in her arms, Emiri looked delighted. "Let's sleep together in my bed."

"No!"

Koga tried to grab the cat from Emiri. To his amazement, Margot's body stretched even further, making it difficult to lift her completely out of Emiri's arms. With some effort, he managed to hoist her up.

"I got this cat. It's *my* cat, so she will sleep with *me*."

"What?" Emiri frowned.

Natsue furrowed her brow. "Come on—you don't have to be so selfish."

"No, no. Margot sleeps in the spare room with me. Right, Margot? Let's sleep together again tonight, okay? Oh yes, Margot, you love Daddy, too? You do. Yes, you do."

Koga refused to let go of Margot.

After dinner and a bath, he retreated with Margot upstairs. The futon and the crumpled robe remained untouched from that morning. He felt a strange sense of satisfaction. *I really surprised them.* It served them right for always sidelining him, the head of the household.

"All right, Margot, you're a good girl. It's now your second day in our home. Today, you'll sleep well, okay?"

Margot looked up with her tea-green eyes. It was as if she understood human language. But Koga was mistaken.

That night, Margot cried incessantly. *Meow, meow, meow.* It was useless to cover his ears or bury his head under the duvet. *Should I kick Margot out of the room? Or should I try to sleep in the bedroom or living room?* But he couldn't do that after having made a big fuss about sleeping with the cat. As a result, Koga went without a wink of sleep for the second night in a row.

He gave Natsue a shock that morning when she saw him in the bathroom.

"You look terrible. If you're not feeling well, maybe you should take the day off work."

Koga groaned. "I have a meeting today, so I can't take the day off. But please take care of Margot for me. I haven't been able to do anything," he replied.

"That's fine, but be careful. You seem shaky."

"I'm okay. I'm okay . . ." Koga laughed, his eyes rolling back.

Meow, meow, meow. I like it! I like it! Red panties, I like it!

Meow, meow, meow. I like that picture! I also like that red bra!

"Sir? Excuse me, sir?"

The voice came from somewhere in the distance. Koga smiled lazily. *It's too loud here. I'm busy liking things right now.* He felt like he was floating on air. He felt so good.

"Sir!"

Someone was shaking his shoulders. Koga's eyes flew open. A station attendant peered into his face.

"Huh?"

"Sir, we've reached the last stop."

"O-oh no," he stammered as he rushed to get off the train.

He stood dumbfounded on the platform of an unfamiliar station. He had meant to get off at the stop after Kyoto Station but appeared to have missed it. Feeling dizzy, he had hopped onto the local train to avoid the crowds on the express—that had been a mistake. He glanced at his watch, worried he might not make it to work on time.

"Huh?"

No, that can't be. He rubbed his eyes. *My eyes must be blurry from sleep deprivation.* But no matter how many times he looked at his watch, it said the same thing. The large clock in the station indicated that it was past ten o'clock. He had traveled through Kyoto to Osaka and ended up in Hyogo Prefecture. He was seriously late for work.

He could see the blue sky from the platform, and the sun shone brightly upon him. This made sense; the sun was already high in the sky. He gazed up for a while, but time wasn't going to turn back. With resolve, he made a call to his office. He had no choice but to lie about having to take the morning off due to a sudden health problem.

What a disgrace. And it's all because of that quack doctor. Clenching his jaw in frustration, he boarded the express train back to Kyoto. He needed to give that doctor a piece of his mind. He transferred trains and dashed through

Kyoto's narrow streets to reach Nakagyō Kokoro Clinic for the Soul.

Chitose sat at the reception window, looking unconcerned.

"Mr. Koga, we provided you with a ten-day course of cat to take."

"'Ten-day course'? You're speaking about it like it's actual medication." Koga gritted his teeth. "I know I'm also to blame for getting carried away, but thanks to Margot, I haven't been able to sleep at all."

"If you wish to change the cat, please speak with the doctor. Please proceed to the examination room."

Koga swallowed his words in frustration at the nurse's curt response. He didn't like cold people like her. With a heavy heart, he walked into the examination room.

The curtains flew open and the young doctor entered, smiling.

"Hello, Mr. Koga. Seems like you got some good sleep."

"What?" Koga had cooled off somewhat, but he felt his anger bubble up at the doctor's lighthearted attitude. "What are you talking about? For two days, that cat has kept me awake with her constant meowing, and I couldn't sleep a wink!"

"Not a wink, you say?"

"Yes, not a wink!"

"That's strange," the doctor said, cocking his head in contemplation. "Mr. Koga, your hair is disheveled, your clothes are wrinkled, and there are traces of drool around your mouth. Given your appearance, I'd have thought you'd been sound asleep until just a moment ago. Your complexion looks good, as if you're well-rested . . . But I see, not a wink of sleep in two days. Is that right?" The doctor kept tilting his head in disbelief.

Koga stood mouth agape at the doctor's observation of his disheveled, just-woken-up appearance. He should have looked in the mirror in the train station restroom before coming here. It was true that for several hours on the train, he had been lulled into a slumber so comfortable it made up for the sleep deprivation he had experienced over the past couple of days.

"How about your dreams?"

Koga was startled by the doctor's question. "Wh-what do you mean?"

"Your dreams. You mentioned that you always heard someone's voice in your dreams. Did the cat help you with that?" the doctor asked casually.

"That's . . ."

Come to think of it, because he had been kept awake for the last two nights, he hadn't been haunted by dreams. Before coming to the clinic, he had been plagued daily by nightmares of Hinako's high-pitched *I like its* accompanied by mocking and scornful laughter.

The dream he'd had on the train had been unusually pleasant. He had been giving people thumbs-ups and *I like its* without resistance. Natsue, Emiri, Hinako, and the call center workers had all appeared in his dream. They had all smiled with delight as Koga voiced his approval.

Koga remained silent; the doctor tilted his head again.

"Hmm, if you insist, we can prescribe you another cat." The doctor started typing on his keyboard. "We currently have another cat with the same therapeutic effect at our clinic."

"Um, well . . ."

"Yes?"

"Isn't it cruel to replace a cat so quickly just because it's not working?" Koga asked.

"Is it? But if something's not working, it's only natural to replace it. There are plenty of alternatives, you know." The doctor said this with a smile, as if it were the most obvious thing in the world.

Koga couldn't tell whether the doctor was referring to the cat, the medication, or HR issues. Nonetheless, his words struck a chord. As the doctor resumed typing, Koga felt a sudden rush of panic.

"Please let me keep that cat until the end. My wife and

daughter have also grown fond of Margot, so I'd like to leave things as they are. I can put up with sleep deprivation for another eight days or so."

"Understood. We'll keep you on the same cat, but let's adjust how you're taking it. I'll write you a new prescription, so please pick it up from the reception window on your way out."

Koga took the piece of paper from the doctor and left the examination room. The waiting area was empty.

"Mr. Koga," the nurse called out from the reception window.

He handed her the prescription, and in return, she gave him another paper bag. Inside was a worn-out cushion.

"What's this?"

"That's the bed the cat usually sleeps in. When you return the cat, please bring this along, too. Please make sure not to forget it."

Her manner was unfriendly, but she made clear that the bed was important. She was much younger than Koga, but her demeanor put him on edge.

With the cushion in hand, Koga headed to the call center for the afternoon. He made it in time for the meeting, but he received audible sighs from Fukuda and concerned inquiries about his health from Hinako, which embarrassed him.

When he returned home, his gloomy mood dissipated. Natsue and Emiri were laughing in the living room—without him, as always—but Margot was there, too. They turned to Koga with the same smiles they wore for Margot. The atmosphere felt distinctly different from usual.

Margot had been lying stretched out on the floor, but she rose and made her way to Koga's feet.

"Oh, Margot. Aren't you a good cat, coming to greet your master like this?" Koga let out a proud snort.

But when Margot caught a whiff of Koga's feet, her eyes widened, her mouth fell open, and she stood frozen with a look of utter shock that said, *Your feet are so stinky, I'm stupefied!* Even humans don't display such blatant expressions.

"What kind of face are you making, huh?"

"That's called the flehmen response." Emiri held up her phone. "It seems animals do that when they smell something. Margot, do it one more time. Dad, let Margot smell your feet."

"No, I don't want to. My feelings are hurt. She's acting like my feet stink." *How rude.*

Curious, Koga smelled his own socked feet. After a day sweating in leather shoes, his feet emitted a pungent odor.

"Yikes! This is bad. No wonder the cat was horrified."

"The reaction has nothing to do with smelliness. It's

how animals check out what they're dealing with," explained Emiri. "Dad, move your feet. I'm going to take a video of Margot."

"Why?"

Even though he was being treated like an obstacle, he was thrilled Emiri was speaking to him. As for Margot, she was showing interest in the paper bag from the clinic. He pulled out a boxy pale pink bed. Its fabric was pilled, as if worn from repeated washings.

"What's that? It looks worn-out," asked Natsue.

"A cat bed. This little one can't sleep at all at night, so I thought maybe she'd sleep on this. Come on, Margot. I got you your bed."

Margot brought her nose to the bed. Her eyes widened again and her mouth fell open in shock.

"Perfect! Margot, hold that expression!" said Emiri, pointing her phone at the cat and snapping a picture. "Dad! Your feet! Get them out of the way!"

"What's going on?"

Koga quickly moved his feet. Margot was already sitting primly, as if nothing had happened.

"Ugh. I did get a cute pic, but your socks are in the shot. Maybe I can edit them out. Or maybe it's funnier with them in. 'Margot makes a stinky face at Dad's socks . . .'" Emiri chuckled as she typed on her phone.

Koga was happy that a picture of him made his daughter laugh, even if it was an unauthorized shot of his socked feet. Natsue, too, was smiling as she watched their exchange.

Emiri scooped up Margot, laid her down on the floor, and stroked her belly.

"Hey, Dad. Do you know why she's called Margot?"

"Because the instruction leaflet said so."

"No, I mean the origin of her name. Look at these white circular patches. There are two on her belly, at the base of her legs." She turned the cat over to show her back to Koga. "And more on her butt and back. Five white spots in total. And what's the word for 'circle'? *'Maru.'* And what's the word for 'five'? *'Go.' Maru-go*. Margot!"

"That's just a coincidence. Besides, the spots don't look like circles at all."

"No, that's definitely it. They were probably originally much more circular, and then she grew and the spots stretched."

"Is that so?"

"That's right."

It had been years since the three had laughed together about the same thing. Finding common ground in what they found cute, Koga felt he had regained something.

"A fart in a windstorm," he muttered. The cat, which

he'd thought would be of no use whatsoever, seemed to have brought about some change.

Natsue frowned. "Jeez, did you fart? Go away."

"I swear I didn't!" When he looked over at Margot, he saw that her eyes and mouth were wide open. "What's with that face, Margot?"

Emiri grimaced and covered her nose with her hand. "Ew, it stinks. Margot, let's go over there."

"There's no stink! I didn't fart. What's wrong with all of you?"

Emiri carried Margot upstairs, and Natsue retreated to the kitchen. Just a moment ago, things had been cheerful, but in the blink of an eye, Koga found himself alone in the living room.

From that night on, following the instructions in the new leaflet, they left all the doors ajar, and Margot began sleeping in various places throughout the house. She curled up in the pink bed in the living room, crawled into Emiri's futon, and squeezed herself into the small gap between Natsue's pillow and the mattress.

All that was rather endearing, but when she came to sleep near Koga, she clung to him tightly. She would perch herself on his chest, and no matter how many times he removed her, she would climb back up. She was, of course, heavy. When it became too uncomfortable to breathe, he would turn onto his stomach, but then she'd climb onto his back. When he moved her again, she'd wedge herself into his armpit, making it impossible for him to roll over.

Left with no choice, Koga had to fall asleep with his body straight like a rod and his arms crossed over his chest. Margot would then sprawl under Koga's chin, slowly crushing his throat. When he awoke in the morning, his mouth would be filled with fur.

The previous night, Margot had pulled down the coat he had left draped on a chair and curled up in it. He had intended to wear the coat to work, but it was now covered in cat fur, and once again, he became the source of his family's amusement.

"Doesn't it seem like this cat is out for me?" said Koga.

"I posted that pic of you in your fur-covered clothes, and it exploded with likes," said Emiri. "Cats really rule the Internet. The number of views was off the charts."

In the past, whenever they were finished with dinner, everyone went off to their own rooms, but ever since Margot had arrived, they'd started gathering where she was. Emiri was recording a video of Margot on her phone.

Koga was crawling on the carpet, trying to take a good video on his phone as well, but Emiri's words made him flinch. "I don't get why it's all about the likes. Listen, Emiri—cheap compliments are worthless."

"You don't get it, Dad."

"What do you mean?"

"Complimenting someone can be tricky."

Emiri also got down onto the carpet and began filming Margot from another angle. Koga looked at the image of Margot on his phone, feeling miffed.

"That's not true. It's easy enough to give a compliment. All you have to do is say you like someone's outfit or hairstyle or something."

"That's risky, Dad. It's a fine line."

"What do you mean?"

With phones in hand, they spoke to each other, Margot lying prostrate between them. Their eyes were glued to their screens.

"People can tell from your gaze or the way you speak if you really like something or if you're being superficial. Complimenting someone's outfit is the trickiest. If you're not careful, they'll think you're making fun of them, or, in your case, Dad, the wrong words could be taken as sexual harassment."

"S-sexual harassment?"

It was a term that struck fear into the hearts of middle-aged male managers. He wanted to believe he had managed to cover up the incident with the red lingerie the other day.

"Besides, even if you genuinely mean it, it takes energy to compliment people. When you're feeling down, even just tapping your phone screen can feel like a chore. Like, especially when I'm sent videos I have no interest in, I'm irritated. But I can't ignore them, so I sometimes reluctantly leave comments."

"How grown-up of you," said Natsue.

Emiri shrugged. "Well, I guess it goes both ways. Everyone wants to show off the things they love and receive compliments for them. If both parties can find happiness in that exchange, even cheap compliments and likes have value. Dad, why don't you show pictures of Margot to the ladies at work? Cats are powerful."

Emiri was smiling. Koga, while amazed by his daughter's mature insight, felt like he had received a light slap on the wrist.

At the call center, at lunchtime, it was business as usual, with Hinako amiably listening to the staff members brag about various accomplishments. Koga no longer felt irritated while watching her smile and praise others. Rather, he was impressed by her thoughtful responses. His nightmares and insomnia seemed to have disappeared without warning, but he didn't solely credit the cat for this. He had finally let go of his baseless fixation, and Hinako's voice no longer echoed in his mind.

That day, he spotted something unusual: Hinako was taking a break alone in a secluded hallway that used to serve as the smoking area. Her back was turned to him and she was looking out the window.

After confirming there was no one else around, Koga approached her.

"Ms. Nakajima."

Hinako turned around. "Oh, Mr. Koga."

"Check this out." Koga timidly took out his phone. "It's a video I took at home, if you'd like to see it. I find it kind of soothing."

"I didn't think your child was still young." Hinako smiled wearily, then quickly took a sharp breath. "I'm sorry. I didn't mean for it to come out that way. I'm a bit distracted right now. Is it a video of your child? Please, I would love to see it."

Hinako wore her usual bright smile. When she saw the video on Koga's phone, her smile grew wider.

"Oh, a cat! I didn't know you had a cat."

In the video, Margot was asleep, stretched out on her

back like a human, with her front paws crossed over her chest and her tail extended between her hind legs. It was the same sleeping position Koga had adopted to stop Margot from sleeping on his chest.

Hinako laughed. "Does she really sleep like that?"

"Yes. Doesn't she look like Tutankhamun's sarcophagus?"

"So adorable! I like it!" Hinako laughed loudly. Her laughter was brighter than usual as she watched the video with wide eyes.

As Emiri had said, it took energy to compliment people. Hinako had come from Tokyo to lead a large team and was expected to deliver results. Yet the middle-aged men around her were uncooperative and cynical. She must have occasionally felt tired and wanted to be alone. There were undoubtedly times when she didn't want to praise people.

"Animals really do bring comfort, don't they?" said Hinako. Sure enough, her smile seemed slightly weary. "I like children and babies, too. But I live alone, and sometimes I don't know how to react. Well, I guess my reactions don't matter anyway."

"Everyone is delighted by your reactions." Before he knew it, the sincere words had dropped out of Koga's mouth. "Your compliments bring people joy. I think that's great."

For a moment, Hinako looked taken aback, but then she smiled shyly.

"Oh, my. *I've* been given a compliment. You're right. It does feel nice."

Emiri was right. It does take energy to do something if you're not used to it. But if it makes someone this happy, offering praise here and there is a small price to pay.

"There's also this clip. Take a look."

When Koga shared with Hinako the picture of Margot's flehmen response, she returned to her usual upbeat self and gushed about the cat's cuteness. He understood why people gravitated to Hinako. It was like how his family was drawn to Margot. The simple joy warmed his heart.

Inside the glass-walled booth, kittens were frolicking with one another. All the cats were fluffy, each as cute as a plush toy. However, the prices on the display were far from cute.

Perhaps because it was a holiday, the pet store in the shopping mall was teeming with families with young children. The store was vibrant and spacious, with puppies darting around in their enclosures and kittens enjoying ample space to roam. Some cats were playing, while others, paying no mind to the customers pressed against the glass, snoozed.

Every store attendant held a cat or a dog and, upon

making eye contact, would immediately allow customers to pet them. *Too tempting,* thought Koga. He made sure not to get too close to any of them.

Emiri placed her hand against the glass, gazing at the kittens inside. A light brown long-haired kitten with sapphire blue eyes caught her attention.

"Hey, Mom, isn't this one beautiful?"

"Yeah, it is. But remember, we were told the Scottish fold is a good breed. There's one over here, although its ears don't have the typical charming fold."

Initially, Koga had been examining the cats in earnest, but he quickly grew weary. The variety of breeds, the complicated names, and the high prices were beyond his imagination. He sat alone on a sofa in the store while Emiri and Natsue chatted with the staff.

It was Natsue who had suggested getting a cat. It was right after Margot had been returned. Even though Margot had been with them for only ten days, she had left a significant impression on the family and had transformed the atmosphere. Natsue had spent the most time with Margot at home during the day. It was understandable why she was overwhelmed by a sense of loss.

Koga recalled what had happened when he returned Margot. Before handing over the pet carrier in the examination room, he had asked the doctor a question.

"Um, will you be sending Margot to a good place?"

"Yes?" The doctor tilted his head.

"My wife's concerned. She said that while Margot's bed is old, it looks like it's been washed many times, so she must be cared for by a nice person who values her favorite things. Is that true?"

"Oh, yes, that's right. Cats don't care about the cost of things; they only care if the scent is to their liking. Rest assured; she belongs to a home where she can enjoy a good night's sleep without concern."

The doctor's response had been casual and somewhat flippant, but he handled the carrier gently. Margot didn't seem the least bit reluctant to part from Koga. In fact, there was a calm and cool look of relief in her clear, tea-green eyes.

There were no cats with mottled fur here. No adult cats either. Koga liked strong cats like Margo, but he felt there was something wrong with the act of selecting a cat.

"Hey, Dad."

Emiri and Natsue approached him. It seemed that they had made a decision. With some effort, Koga got up.

"Don't worry about the price. Pick out a cat you guys like. I can wait on buying a new car until after the next vehicle inspection."

"It's not that," Emiri said. She glanced around the shop, a complicated look crossing her face. "There are so many cute cats here and plenty of customers, too. I'm sure these cats will find a good home without our help. So instead of a kitten from a pet shop, what do you think about this?"

Emiri showed him her phone. Initially, he thought he was looking at the website of a different store, but he quickly realized his mistake.

"A cat shelter?"

"Yeah. A friend from college adopted a cat from there. They're having an open house today. Can we go?"

"Shelter cats, huh?" Koga wondered how a shelter was different from the pound. Weary of the bustle of the pet shop, he agreed to visit the shelter as Emiri suggested.

City Cat Rescue Center, operated by an animal welfare organization, was located in a quiet area a short distance from the city center. Although it was housed in a nondescript building that reminded one of a big-box store, the atmosphere was not as bleak as he had imagined. It was spacious and bright inside. Animal enclosures lined the walls with cats on view for visitors.

"There are so many cats here. Were they all abandoned?"

"They're here for various reasons. Some were rescued; others were abandoned by their owners."

"Abandoned, huh? People can do terrible things."

While Emiri and Natsue crouched down to examine each cat, Koga wandered around the shelter. There were many cats, and not just in the visitors' area. Some were in cages with tags that said they were under treatment or not available for adoption. Unlike the sleek-furred, bright-eyed cats he'd seen earlier, these bore scars on their faces, had uneven fur, and exhibited other signs of hardship.

When he returned, Emiri and Natsue were taking another look at the first enclosure.

"These are all adult cats. You're okay with that?" he asked.

"Kittens are cute, but they come with their own challenges. I'm a bit worried because we've never had a cat or a dog before."

"But can adult cats form bonds with their new owners?"

"They can," said a voice from behind them.

Koga turned around.

"Hey! What are you doing here?"

It was the peculiar doctor from the clinic, sporting that same thin smile that Koga knew all too well. But instead of his white lab coat, he was wearing Wellington boots. In his arms was a dark-colored cat.

"Do you work here? Oh, I see. You're also a vet. That's why you have a cat."

"Huh?" The man tilted his head. It was the same playful gesture he'd displayed at the clinic. "I'm Kajiwara, the deputy director of this shelter. Regarding your question, all our cats up for adoption are super friendly. With time and care, they'll warm up to you. Have you ever had a cat before?"

Nudging Koga aside, Emiri responded. "No. We recently took care of a cat for a short while. She was so ridiculously cute. It made us want to get our own."

"I see. That's fate for you. Our adoption requirements are relatively lenient. Many shelters won't allow pets to be adopted by people who live alone or families without prior experience with pets, but our policy is about opening more doors to adoption."

Emiri seemed smitten by Kajiwara's friendly smile. Koga stared at the man. *He's definitely that doctor. His appearance, the way he talks, his friendly but somewhat distant smile—all exactly the same.*

The cat in Kajiwara's arms squirmed and turned its face toward them. Its eyes were light green, similar to Margot's. There was a large black patch on one side of its nose, and on the other side there was a patch with an irregular pattern of stripes. Its coat was somewhat speckled.

"Is that a tortoiseshell cat?" Koga asked.

"Since there's a lot of white in her coat, I'd say she's more of a calico. There might be some tabby mixed in there, too. She's female, about three years old."

"Is she up for adoption?"

"Yes. She's well-behaved, but as you can see, her facial markings aren't very appealing, so she's not popular. Right, my dear?" Kajiwara spoke kindly to the cat.

The cat lifted her nose and leaned her face toward him. Koga, Emiri, and Natsue were all staring at the cat. There were many felines at the facility that were more beautiful and charming, but for some reason, they were all captivated by the one in Kajiwara's arms.

"Has she already been given a name?" Emiri asked.

"The cats here have numbers as names, which I guess is a bit boring. This one's in the sixth cage, so we call her Six. After adoption, the owner is welcome to give the cat a new name. How about it? Want to hold her for a bit?"

"May I?"

"Here." Kajiwara handed Emiri the cat. She held the cat awkwardly and flashed a troubled smile at her parents.

"Oh wow, she's so warm."

The cat lifted its nose again. Emiri broke into a wide grin as she watched the cat sniff the air.

"Since she has so many patches and is in the sixth enclosure, let's call her Six-Patch," said Koga.

Emiri frowned. "Dad, that's not fair. You can't decide on her name on your own."

"Huh? Well, I didn't mean to—"

"I wanted to give her a cuter name, like Mocha or Berry," said Emiri.

"Then name her Mocha or Berry."

"But now I can only see her as Six-Patch. Right, Mom?"

"You're right. She looks like a Six-Patch." Natsue leaned in toward the cat and laughed. The cat glanced nervously between them.

"If you're interested in this little one, you can take her for a trial stay for a few days to confirm compatibility. There are a few simple documents you need to review," said Kajiwara, gesturing toward the reception desk.

Natsue and Emiri headed over together. The cat was once again in Kajiwara's arms. It seemed this patchy cat was coming home.

Koga's gaze kept flicking to Kajiwara's face.

"Um, are you sure you're not the doctor from the clinic? You know, the small practice called Nakagyō Kokoro Clinic for the Soul, located between Takoyakushi and Rokkaku streets?"

"Oh, I know that place," said Kajiwara with a laugh. "It's Dr. Kokoro's hospital, right? I used to go there quite often. He also drops by our rescue center occasionally."

"When you say hospital, you mean a psychiatric clinic, right?"

"Psychiatric clinic? No, I'm talking about Suda Animal Hospital in Nakagyō Ward."

Their conversation wasn't quite clicking. Even Kajiwara looked troubled and was laughing awkwardly.

Emiri and Natsue returned.

"We decided to take Six—I mean, this cat—home for a trial stay. Is that okay, Dad?"

"Yeah."

Koga was distracted. He was looking at the ID badge hanging from the man's neck. *Tomoya Kajiwara*. He looked just like that doctor from the clinic but more composed. Talking to him like this, he did seem like a different person.

Kajiwara handed the cat to Emiri. "Six, make sure you get along with everyone," he said, scratching the cat's head.

The cat closed her eyes in apparent contentment. Emiri was in high spirits as she placed the cat into the pet carrier borrowed from the shelter.

"When I uploaded a pic with a caption that we're trial fostering a cat, I got a ton of likes. Hey, people are saying they like the name Six-Patch. I don't know why, Dad, but the name's popular. Good for you."

"Hmph. Your father isn't easily delighted by cheap compliments."

But truthfully, he was glad the name he had given the cat was getting likes. Although not a tortoiseshell, it seemed a cat that was strong like Margot was joining their household. That, too, brought him joy.

Once I get home, I'll take some videos and photos, too. Then I'll share them with people. And if people compliment me for them, I'll compliment them back. Six-Patch is sure to get a ton of likes. Essentially, that means I will get all the likes for naming her.

Koga grinned as he watched his wife and daughter shower the cat with adoration.

Koyuki

3

Koyuki

Megumi Minamida stopped by the park on the corner of Rokkaku and Fuyacho streets. When she turned around, she saw her daughter, Aoba, standing on the other side of the street, gazing down at her feet. Irritation started to bubble up. She breathed out slowly and reminded herself to stay calm.

"Aoba, hurry up. You're getting in the way of other people."

Aoba approached her with a sullen look. For a fourth grader, she still looked quite babylike and exuded an air of sadness, so it made Megumi feel like a villain for being cold to her. But having been forced to go on this wild-goose chase, Megumi didn't have the bandwidth to be kind. They had indeed found a hospital located at the vague address

Aoba's friend had given her, but it wasn't the one they were looking for.

"Lize and Tomomi said it's around here. Kiko's mom's friend also said they've been seeing Dr. Kokoro at his practice," said Aoba.

"We were just there, and it was a different hospital, wasn't it?" Megumi couldn't hide the frustration in her tone even though she knew it was also her fault for not looking up the details ahead of their visit.

When Aoba got to the fourth grade, she became markedly more difficult to deal with. While it was normal for her to complain that school was boring or her studies were tough, recently she'd started exhibiting signs of depression. And a few days ago, she expressed her desire to visit Dr. Kokoro's clinic in Nakagyō Ward.

At first, Megumi dismissed the idea of psychiatric care for elementary school students, but when she casually brought up the topic with her neighborhood mom friends, to her surprise they insisted that these days, mental health care was considered normal even for preschoolers. Megumi felt an urgent need to act. If she didn't take Aoba to the clinic right away, she felt she would be seen as an old-fashioned, incompetent mother. She couldn't bear to remain idle.

And so Megumi arrived at Dr. Suda Kokoro's hospital

in Nakagyō Ward, as directed by the map app on her phone. But it wasn't a psychiatric clinic or a pediatric clinic. It wasn't even a clinic for people.

It was an old and smallish hospital, located along a narrow path. In the entrance was a large dog lying down beside a bench. On a wall were hundreds of photographs, all featuring dogs or cats, many with their owners.

Dr. Kokoro's hospital turned out to be an animal hospital. Megumi had reluctantly come here because she wanted to fit in with her mom friends, but she'd made a mistake by unquestioningly accepting Aoba's information.

"Let's go home. Mom needs to prepare dinner," said Megumi.

"No way. I want to find Dr. Kokoro's clinic. It's on some street in Nakagyō Ward." Aoba frowned.

"We passed Suda Animal Hospital. It was a vet."

"It's somewhere different. On the top floor of a building, with a doctor who actually listens to you. Both Lize and Tomomi have their own regular psychiatrists, and they're told that they can call up the doctor anytime, even if there's nothing wrong."

"Regular psychiatrists for children. I see." Megumi laughed weakly. *Her friends are completely manipulating her.*

Megumi had heard from her mom friends that therapy and mental health care were becoming trendy among kids.

Things that kids thought were cool included going to cram school, participating in extracurricular activities, having phones, and seeking advice from professionals instead of their parents or teachers. The older the kids became, the harder Megumi found it to connect with or understand them.

"If there's anything you want to talk about, you can talk to me after you finish your homework."

"You say that, but you don't understand anything, Mom," Aoba said. "You never listen to me."

"Fine—go find this clinic yourself," she snapped, storming away.

As she reached the corner of Tominokoji Street, she turned back and saw that Aoba had come to a halt in front of a store halfway down the block. She was looking at Megumi and pointing.

"Mom, there's a narrow alley over here."

"What are you talking about? There's no path that goes through here."

"But look!" Aoba stomped her feet childishly. "There's a path!"

Megumi walked briskly up to Aoba. "I'm sure it's just a parking lot or something. You can't just walk onto someone's property . . ."

And there, indeed, was an alley. A dimly lit narrow path stretched before them.

"See, I told you. There is an alley. I was right," said Aoba triumphantly.

From the main street, it looked like nothing but a small gap between buildings. It was no wonder they'd missed it, she thought as she peered in. An old building stood at the end of the alley. It gave off a sinister feeling that made her pause. Aoba took off running.

"Mom, I'll go check it out."

"Hey, don't go into that strange building."

"But you said, 'Go find this clinic yourself.'"

Aoba ran cheerfully inside. Megumi hurried after her.

The door to the clinic was awfully heavy. "This door!" complained Megumi. That was off-putting enough, but once inside, they were met by a nurse who avoided eye contact and seemed somewhat crabby. Then, in the examination room, there was only a single chair for the patient, leaving Megumi no choice but to stand.

It was almost five o'clock. If they dawdled any longer, her son—a middle schooler on a growth spurt who thought only about food and always came home with a mountain of laundry from his extracurricular activities—would be home before them.

Megumi had planned to drop by the supermarket but now decided against it. *What do we have in the fridge? That reminds me—what should I bring to next week's tea party with the moms? I've run out of things to bring.* She drifted away in thought. Aoba, on the other hand, was clearly excited to be at the clinic.

"That nurse just now was so beautiful. I feel like I've seen her before somewhere. Maybe she looks like a celebrity."

"Be quiet, Aoba." Megumi shot a look at her daughter. Aoba hung her head.

The curtains flew open and a man in a white lab coat entered. It was Megumi's first time encountering a doctor with such youthful, delicate features.

"Wow. What a surprise. You're such a handsome doctor!" said Aoba cheerfully.

Megumi was shocked to hear her daughter express exactly what she was thinking.

"Aoba, *shhh*, don't be rude." It came out more coldly than Megumi had intended, and Aoba once again looked down at her feet and sulked. She was a mother who scolded her child in front of the psychiatrist. She felt uneasy. In today's world, people made a fuss about the smallest things and labeled it abuse. She glanced over at the doctor.

The doctor was smiling.

"The wrong person's in the chair."

"What?"

"Shouldn't you be sitting? You're the patient, after all."

For a second, Megumi didn't understand what he meant. Then her face turned bright red.

"No, not me. My daughter is the one who'd like to speak with you."

"Oh, really? Your daughter?" The doctor peered into Aoba's face. "She doesn't seem to have any issues. Will you tell me your name and age, miss?"

"Aoba Minamida. I'm ten years old."

"What brings you in today?"

"Well . . ."—Aoba tilted her head and swung her feet—"there's something troubling me at school. Can I talk to you about it?"

"Of course. Please go ahead."

"Do you know what cliques are, Doctor? We have them in my class."

Megumi's eyes widened. "Aoba, don't bother the doctor with such—"

"It's fine," said the doctor. "You know some difficult words! Yes, I know what cliques are. I'm a doctor, after all. So, what's the deal with them?"

"Right now, there are two queen bees in my class, and I have to pick which clique to join. But if I don't choose either, I'll end up with no friends. I'm seriously struggling with this decision. My friends Lize and Tomomi said they've been talking to their psychiatrist about this, so I thought I'd talk to you about it as well." Aoba's tone was bubbly, as if she were discussing cartoons.

Megumi covered her eyes. She'd noticed Aoba had been moody lately and she had brought her here hoping to cheer her up. She never expected her daughter to bring up such frivolous matters.

"Aoba, this isn't the time or place to chat about silly things. The doctor's busy, so please bring up something more serious. This is where you can discuss your worries and concerns."

"Oh, it's all right," the doctor said. "We never intended to be that kind of place, but people started coming here based on some rumor or another. We actually only usually see patients with appointments, but it looks like no one's coming today."

"They don't turn up even though they have an appointment?" asked Aoba.

"Yes. We've been waiting for a while now. I wonder why. Maybe the door is too heavy?" The doctor cocked his head curiously.

What a strange doctor. There was an old-fashioned feel to his thick Kyoto accent, but his attitude was casual, like your average student. Megumi began to feel that they had come to the wrong clinic. In the first place, Aoba's problem was without substance and mostly nonsense.

Aoba looked up at her with a smile.

"Mom, you were furious about the door being heavy."

"You don't have to bring up unnecessary things."

Aoba hung her head. The atmosphere had soured, and Megumi couldn't stay here a moment longer. There was a mountain of things she needed to do back home.

"I'm sorry, Doctor, for bothering you with something so trivial. It seems like my daughter just wanted to visit your clinic. Her elementary school has counselors, so I'll have her meet with them instead."

"My problems are not trivial," Aoba muttered, gazing down at her feet. "Mom, you always say my problems are trivial."

"But they are. Now, let's go home. I have to prepare dinner. I'll listen to your problems about the social ladder or whatever later, okay?"

Aoba didn't move. "Why do you never listen to me, Mom?"

"I do. I always listen to you during meals."

"You don't understand anything. No matter what I say, you always say it's my fault or who cares about something so stupid. I already told you about the cliques, but you told me not to get involved in such pointless things."

"That's . . ."

Did she talk to me about this? Did I say that? Even if she had, there would be no way Megumi would remember. An elementary school student's problems changed constantly, like the flavor of the day. Megumi didn't have time to deal with every single one.

"Hmm. This won't do," said the doctor. He crossed his arms. "The door is heavy, huh? That's not good. Should we give the stronger cat a try? Chitose, can you bring the cat?"

The nurse appeared from behind the curtains, holding a pet carrier.

"Dr. Nikké, are you sure this is okay? There's a chance the patients with scheduled appointments might arrive soon." The nurse frowned in disapproval.

The doctor let out a strained laugh. "If they do come, we'll ask them to wait a little. After all, they've kept us waiting for quite a while, so a little wait shouldn't bother them, right?"

"I've no idea," the nurse said. She placed the carrier down on the table and left the room.

How bossy, thought Megumi. On top of that, she'd made it clear she wanted Megumi and Aoba out of there as soon as possible.

"Mom," Aoba murmured.

Megumi wondered if Aoba was thinking the same

thing, but that didn't seem to be the case. Aoba was pointing at the carrier.

"Look. There's a cat."

"A cat? It can't be. This isn't the vet."

"Look—see?" Aoba exclaimed angrily. "Listen to what I'm saying!"

Megumi stooped down toward the plastic crate. Through a side mesh panel, she saw something white. A tiny cat. Perhaps because its fur stood on end, its coat looked thin and disheveled. It had large eyes and a delicate pink nose. There was a smattering of black fur on one of its ears.

"Yuki . . ." Megumi muttered.

Aoba turned to look at her. "Do you know this cat, Mom?"

"No, but . . . There's no way . . . because she . . ."

Megumi couldn't take her eyes off the cat. It looked like a dandelion seed head that might fly away if you blew on it. The memory of a moment when she had had the very same thought came rushing back to her.

She had been in the third grade at the time.

"Meg! Mami! Quick!"

At Reiko's beckoning, Megumi rushed toward her, her schoolbag swinging wildly behind her.

On their way home after school, they had taken a slightly longer detour from their usual route and stumbled upon an empty lot. Reiko had spotted a cardboard box lying at the far end of a cinder block wall and crouched in front of it. Megumi peered over her friend's shoulder; there she saw a dirty towel, newspaper, and three tiny squirming kittens.

"*Wow*, cats!"

Megumi felt instantly joyous. Although she had petted dogs in the neighborhood before, she had never touched a cat. These cats that she was seeing up close for the first time were as small as stuffed animals.

Mew, mew. They emitted delicate squeaks from their tiny mouths. They already had fangs, but they looked rather flimsy, like plastic.

"So cute!"

The three girls tossed their schoolbags aside and became completely engrossed. The kittens yawned and batted their tiny paws against their heads, looking absolutely adorable. The vacant lot was filled with vibrant yellow dandelions. Some had already turned into fluffy white puffs. The kittens appeared as fluffy as those white puffs.

Reiko was the first to touch the cats; she was the girls' leader, and was bright and smart. She picked up one of the cats—so white and pure—from the box. Their friend

Mami also picked up a cat. With both of her friends' eyes saying *It's your turn*, Megumi nervously picked up the last kitten from the box.

The cat was astonishingly light and soft. Its fur, so fine that it looked like it could be blown away, stood on end. It was almost entirely white except for a hint of black fur on one of its ears. Its nose was a faint shade of pink, while its eyes were large.

For a while, the three girls simply held the cats, but after a while, Reiko stood up.

"I'm going to adopt this cat."

"What?" Megumi and Mami exchanged glances.

"Sure, I'll take it in. I feel bad for them," Reiko said. She looked down at her friends, who were still crouching. "I'll beg my mom to let me keep it. You should both do that, too."

"But . . ." Megumi, with cat still in hand, lowered her head. "I don't think my mom would let me. Our house is small, and all."

"You won't know unless you ask. My mom works, you know. She's a schoolteacher and busier than other moms."

"That's true, but . . ."

There were no pets at Megumi's house. The closest thing was the rhinoceros beetle her little brother had brought home during the summer. Even that was left in an insect box by the front door, and who knew who took care of it. When she imagined her mother's face, she knew there was no way she could bring the kitten home. But Reiko's gaze was bearing down on her.

Mami stood up with determination. "I'll adopt the cat. I'll try asking my mom."

"Mami, that's so nice of you."

"Yeah. I'd feel sorry for these cats if we didn't do anything. If Mom says no, I'll ask Dad."

Megumi felt an invisible alliance forming between Reiko and Mami. She rose to her feet and made her own declaration. "I'll adopt a cat, too. I'll also ask my dad if my mom says no."

"Really? Then let's all take a cat."

"Yeah, that sounds good. Let's all take one."

The joy of being acknowledged by Reiko filled Megumi with courage. The cat was stirring against her chest, but not enough to escape her grasp. Suddenly, she felt a sense of ownership over the cat.

"Hey, how about we name them?"

At Reiko's suggestion, the three of them came up with names for the cats right then and there. Megumi decided to name her cat Yuki because it was, like its name, white as snow. It had some black fur on one of its ears, but Megumi found that endearing.

I'm going to look after Yuki. Megumi cradled the kitten to her chest.

When Megumi arrived home, she discovered that her mother, conveniently, was out. Taking advantage of the moment, she laid out a piece of newspaper inside the foyer and placed Yuki on it. Her younger brother, Yoshihito, who had come home from school earlier, stood at the top of the stairs, gaping in shock.

"Sis, are we getting a cat?"

"Yeah, we are. Isn't she cute? Her name is Yuki."

"Are you sure it's okay? Mom's going to be mad."

Megumi glared at Yoshihito; he looked worried.

"Shut up!" she snapped. "Don't worry, I'm taking care of the cat. You're not allowed to touch her. She's mine."

Yoshihito immediately teared up at his sister's rebuke. Her brother, only a year younger than she, was quick to cry.

"Oh, come on. You're such a crybaby. Here—you can pet her."

"Okay," replied Yoshihito. He stepped into the foyer in his socks and crouched to admire the kitten. "She's so small and cute."

"Right?"

Together they gazed at little Yuki. Yuki was looking up at them, mewling as if she was complaining about something.

They heard a sound outside, and the front door slid open. Their mother, with grocery bags in both arms, was home. Her movements had become clumsy due to her protruding belly. In two months, another brother was going to join them.

Their mother let out a deep sigh. Then, her face turned pale. Her eyes had landed on the cat standing between Megumi and Yoshihito.

"Hey, wait a minute! What's all this?"

Megumi was petrified by her mother's sharp and booming voice. She had anticipated a mild admonition, but Yuki was so cute that she had naively believed her mother would be all smiles. Instead, she had responded with a fierce rejection.

"Go return it. Right now!" yelled her mother, bags still in hand.

"But, Mom, this poor little thing—"

"What were you thinking, bringing home a stray cat? We can't keep it! Take it back to where you found it!" Her mother narrowed her eyes.

It wasn't uncommon for Megumi to be scolded for not doing her homework or for fighting and hitting Yoshihito, but it was the first time she'd seen her mother this furious.

Yoshihito scrunched up his face and let out a loud wail. Megumi wanted to cry, too, but she held back her tears.

"Mom, listen. Reiko found the cats. There were three of them, and Reiko said if she begged her mom, her mom would definitely let her keep the cat, so Mami and I should do the same."

"What does Reiko have to do with this? You brought this cat home, so you have to go return it!"

She ignored the trembling Megumi and headed into the house, pausing only to snap at Yoshihito. "Enough with the tears! You're going to be a big brother soon, so cut it out immediately!"

Yoshihito's cries grew even louder. His bawling drowned out Yuki's soft whimpering. Tears spilled from Megumi's eyes onto the newspaper under her feet. Her mother only continued to frown.

"Go return it to where you found it before it gets dark," said her mother before disappearing into the kitchen.

—•—

Megumi clutched Yuki, wrapped in newspaper, in her arms and slowly made her way to the vacant lot.

Mom is a witch. A mean witch.

Megumi's tears flowed uncontrollably. Yuki was clinging to her clothes with her tiny claws. It was heartless to abandon a small creature so utterly dependent on her.

When she arrived at the empty lot, she found someone

by the cinder block wall. It was Mami, crouching by the box.

"Mami."

Mami turned around, tears streaming down her flushed face. Inside the box was the kitten Mami had brought home.

Megumi crouched down next to her friend. "I guess it didn't work out for you. My family won't let me either."

"Yeah. My mom said, 'When your father gets home, he'll be furious, so go get rid of this now.'"

"Same here. My mom's a witch. I hate her."

"My mom's a witch, too. But Reiko's mom's a schoolteacher, so she wouldn't abandon the kittens. Reiko should've taken all three of them from the beginning. She was the one who found them, after all."

"Yeah, that's true."

Mami's presence significantly comforted Megumi.

After wiping away her tears with her sleeve, Mami stood up. "I have to go home. If I don't practice the piano, my mom's going to get mad at me."

"I'm going home, too," said Megumi. Not wanting to be left behind, Megumi released Yuki into the box. Yuki and the other kitten were now meowing side by side.

"I'm sorry. Bye," Mami blurted out before she dashed away.

Megumi hurried after her. The cardboard box and the dandelions in the empty lot disappeared from sight. She parted ways with Mami and ran straight home.

When she got back, her mother was in the kitchen. With her back to Megumi, she asked, "Where did you leave the cat?"

"In the empty lot on the corner where the cherry blossom tree is."

"I see. I know you have homework. Finish it before dinner."

"I will."

Megumi fled to the living room. She had expected the scolding to continue, but her mother was strangely calm, which only scared her more. She decided to avoid mentioning Yuki any further and get on with finishing her homework.

By dinnertime, her mother had returned to her usual self. She scolded Megumi for leaving carrots on her plate and for eating too slowly. She yelled when she and Yoshihito fought over the TV. Megumi was still reeling from what had happened with Yuki, but when she remembered she had a flute recital at school tomorrow, that took over her thoughts. She was saddened that she had to practice the flute instead of watching her favorite cartoon. Her eyes remained teary the entire time she played.

Her father worked night shifts, so she rarely saw him

except on his days off. It was always just the three of them—her, Yoshihito, and her mother—during meals and bath time. Only when it was time to go to bed, her and her brother's futons laid out side by side in the tatami room, was she alone with Yoshihito.

As Megumi drifted off, she was awoken by a sudden noise. *What is it?* When she turned to look at her brother beside her, she found him fast asleep with his blanket kicked away dramatically. Thinking she might have imagined the sound, Megumi went back to sleep, but after a while she heard it again, this time more clearly. It was the sound of their front door closing. Because their house was old, when the front door slid open or closed, the sound reverberated to the second floor. Someone had come in or gone out.

Is it Dad? She crawled on all fours to the window to look outside, but it was too dark to tell. A chill ran down her spine, and she felt the urge to use the bathroom. Rubbing her sleepy eyes, she made her way downstairs.

It was dark on the ground floor. In the narrow living room at the bottom of the stairs, her mother was sprawled across the desk, her face buried in her arms.

When she called out, "Mom," her mother's shoulders jolted in surprise, and she looked up. It was hard to see in the dim light, but her mother was wiping her cheek with her hand.

"What is it? Going to the bathroom?"

"Yeah."

It was her usual mother, but there was something different about her. She seemed somewhat lonely, and her voice lacked strength. Unease came over Megumi. She felt as if her mother was slipping away, and that scared her.

"Mom, what's wrong?"

"What? Nothing's wrong. Don't talk nonsense. Go back to bed. If Yoshihito kicks off his blanket, make sure to tuck him back in properly. You're his big sister."

It was her usual irritated, fast-talking mother. She felt relieved and angry at the same time. *Nonsense.* Anything Megumi brought up was invariably dismissed the same way.

After using the bathroom, Megumi returned to her futon. Yoshihito was sleeping with his entire belly exposed, and she deliberately turned away.

I hate Mom. She never listens to me, and she's always angry.

Megumi pulled the blanket over her head and squeezed her eyes shut.

"What happened to the cat?"

Megumi's chest tightened at the sound of Aoba's hesitant voice.

Inside the carrier, the kitten was licking its paw, which bore distinct creases between each toe. The paws were disproportionately large for its body, and the imbalance in size was painfully adorable. The kitten, seemingly noticing their attention, stopped moving and stared back at them intently. Its innocent eyes didn't yet know to be cautious.

It couldn't be the same cat. It was almost thirty years since she'd picked up Yuki, then abandoned her a few hours later. And yet they looked exactly alike. Fluffy white fur. The black patch around the ear. The shiny slate blue eyes.

How have I forgotten about it until now? What did I do back then? How cruel I was.

"My memory's hazy about what happened after that. It's likely I did nothing and moved on. I don't even remember what happened to the cats my friends adopted. I have no idea what happened to Yuki and the others."

She retraced her memory in a daze. She was young then, and she hadn't spared any further thoughts about the cat. She was sure she hadn't even bothered to go back to the vacant lot. At least she couldn't remember doing anything like that. How heartless, ignorant, and irresponsible she had been. When she recalled her family's situation at the time, she thought it was no wonder that her mother had been angry.

The meaning of her mother's actions that night was clear to her now. Her mother must have gone alone to check on how the cat was doing. She couldn't adopt it. But she couldn't help but check on it. She couldn't turn a blind eye, not as a parent and not as a human being.

Mew. Mew. In the present, a cat was crying. The cat back then, too, must have been lonesome, hungry, and cold. Without understanding the circumstances, she had taken the cat home. She might not have meant harm, but she had been naive. She saw now how foolish she had been.

The doctor, who had been listening silently, lifted up the carrier. He turned it toward himself and opened the door.

"This is a fast-acting cat," he said, pulling the kitten out from the carrier. He held the cat with one hand on its stomach and used the other to support its hind legs.

"This is how you hold a cat. Their bodies are extremely flexible, so don't be afraid to hold them firmly. Here you go."

"Umm . . ."

The doctor placed the cat in Megumi's arms. His movements were remarkably graceful, and in one fluid motion the cat nestled against Megumi's chest. So small and warm. Megumi also noticed it was slightly larger than Yuki had been. It still had the innocent charm of a kitten, but its body was well-developed. After a few moments, the kitten became restless and began squirming and trying to escape.

"Oh no. What should I do? I'm going to drop the cat."

"Hold on to it tighter. It'll be fine."

"Still . . ."

The kitten resisted being held and tried to break free. Its thin white fur looked less like dandelion fluff and more like an Arctic fox.

"Mom, let me hold it."

Aoba reached out, but Megumi swiftly turned her body and deflected her. There was no way her daughter could handle a cat that was wriggling so vigorously.

"No, you'll drop it," she said, but she herself was fumbling with the cat. The kitten twisted around forcefully, claws clinging to Megumi's clothes.

"Oh!"

The kitten slipped through her hands, but Aoba skillfully caught it.

"Safe!" Aoba held the kitten tightly. "Wow, it's so fluffy and tiny. Can't stay still, huh?" She cradled the kitten, pressing it against her chest. "Am I holding the kitten correctly, Dr. Nikké?"

"Yes, you are. You're good at this."

Aoba looked at the kitten and flashed the broadest smile.

"You're so cute. You're like a baby. It's almost scary how small you are."

Aoba cradled the cat determinedly to her chest with sure hands. The kitten looked up with a curious expression and began to give Aoba's hand flicking licks with its tiny tongue.

"Wow, it feels rough. Mom, the cat's tongue feels funny."

Aoba's smile surprised Megumi. When was the last time she had seen an expression like that on her daughter's face? It wasn't just the smile but how confidently she held the kitten that amazed her. Aoba was actually much better at holding the cat than she was. The kitten could sense this, too, which was why it remained calm. It wasn't Megumi the cat relied on. It was Aoba.

"Hey, Mom, maybe this cat is Yuki's kitten. They look exactly alike, right?" said Aoba innocently as she brought her nose to the cat's.

That's impossible. What nonsense is she saying?

That's the type of thing Megumi would usually say. Aoba was still too young to imagine what fate had awaited Yuki. But even if a miracle had occurred, this kitten had no connection to Yuki. It would have been a miracle if someone had taken in Yuki, and miracles didn't happen.

"Yes, maybe. Just maybe," said Megumi calmly, holding

back her tears. She swallowed the pain that her mother had endured alone, never shedding a tear.

Aoba's face lit up with joy. "I'm sure that's it! Dr. Nikké, do you think this cat is Yuki's kitten?"

"Well, who knows?" the doctor replied, playing dumb. "Cats are audacious and fragile, and have shorter lives than humans. But they multiply and they die out, and, perhaps, they might even return."

"What do you mean by that?" asked Aoba. She tilted her head in confusion.

The doctor chuckled. "Who knows what I mean? Now, how do you feel, Megumi? Any dizziness or nausea?"

"Huh? Uh, no." This doctor was truly odd. He hadn't done anything but smile.

"I see. That's great. It seems like the cat worked well. Cats can solve most problems. But to get a prescription for one, you have to first come to this clinic and open the door yourself. I wish that those who, like you, find the door a tad heavy won't let it bother them and come in anyway. Otherwise, we'll be left waiting around forever."

"Okay . . ." Megumi was still unclear what the doctor was talking about.

The doctor looked at Aoba. "You're concerned about which clique to join; is that right?"

"Yes, that's right!" replied Aoba cheerfully.

The doctor nodded. "It's simple. Choose the clique with the stronger boss. A strong boss has a big face and prominent jaw."

"Prominent jaw?" Aoba raised an eyebrow.

"Yes, it's like everything's squeezed tightly in the middle of the face—the eyes, nose, and mouth. So, which boss has the bigger face?"

Aoba let out a snort. "Well, Lena's face is bigger."

"In that case, you should go with Lena. Now, there seem to be no side effects, so you can go home now. Shall I take the cat?"

The doctor extended his arms, and Aoba reluctantly passed him the cat.

"Dr. Nikké, is this your cat?"

"No, this little one comes from a litter born to someone else's cat. She had a lot of kittens, so they're currently looking for people to adopt them. I think they'll put an ad up on the Internet. They're kittens, so I'm sure they'll find homes quickly."

The doctor placed the cat back in the carrier. The cat let out a meow.

"Now, take care," said the doctor, flashing another smile. He seemed no longer interested.

Is this it? Megumi felt a desperate sense of loss, as if a hole had opened in her chest. Aoba looked up at her.

"Mom, do you think we can adopt this cat?"

Megumi's throat tightened. Taking care of a kitten was no small task. What she didn't know when she was a child, she knew now. Perhaps her mother's decision had been correct. She, an elementary school kid, probably couldn't have managed the responsibility of caring for a cat.

Am I making too abrupt a decision? If she didn't make an effort to listen to her daughter, they would again be swept away by the busyness of everyday life. Just because she couldn't care for a cat, she shouldn't assume Aoba couldn't either.

Megumi asked the doctor, "How much care does this cat need? Does it need to be hand-fed? Does someone need to watch it around the clock?"

"Well, this little one is about two and a half months old. It can eat some solid food, but we're still in the process of weaning it, so it can't eat without help quite yet. You'll need to keep an eye on it while it eats its three meals. It's docile right now, but it's usually quite active. It's definitely a handful, but there's no such thing as a low-maintenance cat."

"Three meals . . ."

Would she be able to feed it after she returned from her part-time job in the afternoon? Would she be able to take care of the cat in the morning rush? Would she be able to give it attention while tidying up in the evening? She pondered, but the answer eluded her. This required more knowledge and preparation. It wasn't a simple decision.

Aoba gently took her hand.

"Mom, I'll do my best to take care of the cat. I'll come straight home from school. I'll wake up early in the morning. I'll look after the cat," Aoba pleaded.

But no matter how serious she was, Megumi couldn't allow it.

"It's better not to have a cat. It'll just be more work for you," the doctor said with a faint smile.

He's right. Megumi looked down and bit her lip. *Yuki, I'm sorry I abandoned you back then. I'm really sorry.*

After a pause, Megumi said, "Please let us adopt this cat. We'll do our best to give it a loving home."

"Yes, but—"

"Please. I'll take care of the cat." Megumi bowed deeply.

"They say cats are capricious, but human beings are much more unpredictable."

Megumi couldn't see the doctor's expression, but from his voice, she sensed that he saw through everything.

Aoba got up and stood beside her mother.

"Dr. Nikké, *I* will be in charge of the cat. I'll take good care of it, so please let us take it home." She bowed like her mother.

"Is that so? In that case, please go to reception for a

rundown on precautions and things to note. And if things don't work out, please come back here."

When the doctor leaned in close to the pet carrier, the prone cat lifted its nose. They held each other's eyes. "You should go. You'll be fine. And you have a place to come back to."

It seemed that the cat and human understood each other. The doctor passed the cat carrier to Aoba. "Here you go." Aoba accepted the carrier with both hands.

As they exited the examination room, the nurse called out to her from the reception window. The nurse had the same blunt attitude as before. She handed Megumi a paper bag.

"What's this?" Megumi asked, looking inside.

"That's stuff the cat was using. There are only the essentials in there, so you'll need to buy the rest. Is there a veterinary hospital near your place? It's better to find a vet that's open late."

"Oh, if I remember correctly, Suda Animal Hospital accepts emergency cases. Do you know it? We actually went to that hospital by accident before coming here."

"Oh yes . . ." The nurse looked down at her feet. "I know it. It's Dr. Kokoro's clinic. Dr. Nikké and I are grateful to him for all his help. If you see Dr. Kokoro, please tell him Chitose sends her regards. Take care now." Her unfriendly demeanor still lingered, but there had been a hint of melancholy in her voice.

Megumi didn't comment. It was better to consult an expert on pet care. Tomorrow, they'd go to Suda Animal Hospital.

When they emerged from the clinic, the cold, dimly lit hallways were as quiet as when they had arrived.

Still clutching the carrier with both hands, Aoba said, "Mom, I just remembered where I've seen that woman."

"Huh?"

"I saw her at Kazusa's dance practice. Um, what was it that she did . . . Japanese traditional dance? I visited Kazusa at her dance studio once, and that lady was there. She had her hair done up like a maiko, a geisha in training, and was wearing a light cotton kimono, but she looked just like that nurse."

"Um . . ." Out of habit, Megumi almost told Aoba to stop talking nonsense. "I don't think a maiko can also be a nurse."

"Hmm, I don't know. They looked so similar, but maybe they're different people." Aoba tilted her head.

A man strolled toward them from the other end of the hallway. He wore a flashy shirt and looked somewhat shady. Megumi turned her head away, making sure not to meet his eye, but as he passed by, he blatantly looked over in their direction. She tried to urge Aoba to walk quickly, but before they could get away, the man called out to them.

"Are you guys looking to rent that empty unit?"

His forehead wrinkled with suspicion and an arrogant look shone in his eye. Megumi was confused. By "empty unit," was he referring to the clinic they had just left?

"That's not an empty unit. It's a mental health clinic," she said.

"That unit's been vacant for years. They say it's jinxed, so even when it gets rented out, tenants leave immediately."

"Mom, what does 'jinxed' mean?"

The man chuckled unkindly. "Kiddo, you know what a 'stigmatized property' is? Well, something scary happened in that unit, and it's now haunted by ghosts."

"Ghosts?"

"That's right. I've heard people say they can hear voices and see spirits. So if you guys rent that unit, don't say I didn't warn you."

He walked into the unit next door. Curious, Megumi looked at the door and saw a plate that read JAPAN HEALTH AND SAFETY ASSOCIATION. The dodginess of its name made her cheeks twitch.

"Mom, he said ghosts . . ." Aoba sounded nervous.

"I'm sure it was a joke. That guy was weird. Now, let's

go. Your brother's probably home already. And we have to feed the cat, too."

"Yup." Aoba's face lit up. She glanced down at the pet carrier, held tightly in her arms like treasure. "Since this kitten is Yuki's child, why don't we name her Koyuki—Little Yuki?"

Megumi nodded silently. Challenging days lay ahead, but she was determined to face them with her daughter.

"Hey, Aoba. Will you tell me about the cliques and the social ladder again?"

"Hmm . . ." Aoba scrunched up her face. "I've told you about them so many times."

"Just once more. This time I'll listen."

"All right, I guess I can." Aoba sighed with a hint of attitude. She then glanced at Megumi. "So, how about you spill the beans on your mom friends gatherings."

"What?"

"Because you always look so gloomy before leaving to see your mom friends. I know deep down you don't want to go."

Megumi was flustered by how accurately her daughter had pinpointed her feelings. "What are you talking about? That's not true."

"Well, I guess it is what it is. Cliques and mom friends are unavoidable social experiences. You know, Koyuki, being human is tough." Aoba addressed the kitten in the carrier and strode ahead.

What did I just hear? thought Megumi. The girl holding the carrier was still young, but she had matured without Megumi's noticing.

"Mom, hurry up!"

Aoba was waiting for her at the end of the narrow path between the buildings. Megumi tutted before hurrying to catch up with her daughter and their new family member.

Akira Shiina, the president and sole member of the Japan Health and Safety Association, was climbing the stairs to the fifth floor. His steps were light, and his breathing remained steady. Despite everything, he was the president of a company that championed health. To verify the effectiveness of the magnetic antiaging necklaces he sold, he never skipped out on exercise.

For a man in his late thirties, his skin was radiant and his body was toned. With the magnetic necklace selling well, it was about time to move out of this rundown building and expand the business. The Nakagyō Building, despite its grand-sounding name, was tucked away in an isolated spot that got no sunlight and didn't have an elevator even in this day and age.

To make matters worse, the unit next door was said to be cursed. By the time Shiina had moved in two years ago, there was no trace of any shadiness, but an unpleasant smell had tickled his nostrils the first time he had stepped onto the fifth floor. No tenant seemed to stick around in the unit. He was convinced that there might be ghosts.

People seemed to come and go from the unit. He'd seen people at the door a few times. They didn't seem like real estate agents, nor did they look like they were on company business.

"What a creepy unit," muttered Shiina as he climbed the stairs.

The mother and daughter he'd seen last week had mentioned something about a clinic. He knew he was being nosy, but while they were speaking, he'd peered into the carrier the daughter was holding. There had been a small white kitten inside.

A chill had gone down his spine. He had heard the unit's history from the real estate agent. It couldn't be that something similar was happening again. If that was the case, he couldn't be next door any longer. He wasn't particularly an animal lover, but the heinous acts of the criminal dealers made him sick.

He reached the fifth floor and stepped into the hallway and was making his way to his office at the end. Just next to his office was the jinxed unit, and a woman—willowy and pale—was standing outside.

A shiver crawled over his skin. As he passed her, he stole a glimpse. Her bangs were neatly pinned up, while the rest of her hair was loosely pulled back. She was no ordinary woman. *She's absolutely stunning.*

The woman stood solemnly in front of the door, her eyes down.

Just as he was closing the door to his office, he heard the woman speak.

"Come back. Come back, my little Chitose."

Her voice was faint and tinged with tears.

He shut the door and shuddered.

"Creepy . . ."

The neighboring unit had to be haunted. He was seriously considering moving out now. It would only be a matter of time before trouble came his way.

Tank and Tangerine

4

Tank and Tangerine

On the ground floor of the shop, ladies' handbags designed by Tomoka were neatly displayed. The production of those bags took place in the office-cum-atelier on the second floor.

"I can't keep it up anymore," said a retail assistant with tears in her eyes.

Not again, thought Tomoka Takamine as she furrowed her brow. She hated talking to emotional people. It was a waste of time, and frankly, she wasn't in the mood to console anyone anyway. She compensated her assistants with salaries that matched their workload and the pride they took in their job, so any complaints were simply selfish.

"I can't keep it up either," another voice chimed in. It was the office assistant.

The employees were both in their early twenties, had studied design to some extent, and had eagerly applied to work there. Yet, just because she'd been a little hard on them, they were now whining. She'd had enough of this.

Still, to have two people revolt at the same time would disrupt the shop's work. On top of wholesale orders, they also accepted custom orders, and their delivery deadlines were approaching.

Tomoka sighed. She was going to win this argument and shut them up. But before she could, someone else, the senior assistant in charge of design, spoke up.

"I can't do this either."

"What?" Tomoka was taken aback by the unexpected third complaint. "Let's all take a breather. What's going on all of a sudden?"

"It's not sudden at all. I can't deal with your perfectionism anymore. Consider today my last day."

"Last day? Are you seriously quitting, just like that?"

"If the senior assistant is quitting, I'm quitting, too."

"Then I'm quitting, too." The two who had begun this whole conversation chimed in.

Before she could stop them, all three left the office.

Alone, Tomoka was left in a daze. It was already pitch-black outside. The space was brightly lit, and she could see her entire body reflected in the glass.

"Oh, boy." Tomoka heard a voice and saw her business partner, Junko, enter the room. "Three people quitting at once is tough. What do you think? Should we give in and ask them to come back?"

Tomoka was annoyed. "We're not going to give in. The way those kids work is just so sloppy and careless."

"Even so, no one can keep up with your obsessive perfectionism."

Tomoka had met Junko in college. They had both aspired to become designers. While Junko had faced setbacks in design, she had excelled in accounting and business management. At the age of twenty-nine, they started a company together and opened a store in Kyoto. It had been almost three years since they'd started.

Tomoka's store on Sakaimachi Street, a popular place to drop by while on a leisurely stroll, was gaining repeat customers of late, and they also had long-term customers who came from far away. This was all thanks to their working late into the night to create quality products. It wasn't a question of her perfectionist principles.

"I'm not asking for perfection," Tomoka snapped. "I just want things done the right way. Within the realm of common sense, of course. What's wrong with being particular about materials and processes? After all, it's their job to minimize costs and source materials efficiently. Anyone can understand that . . ." She felt a pain in the pit of her stomach from getting worked up.

Seeing Tomoka double over, Junko said, "See? You're tormenting yourself with that 'doing things the right way' attitude. Your energy has been spinning out of control recently. You need to relax a little."

"Relax? How do I do that? If I take a break, this small store will go out of business in no time."

"Instead of taking a break, what if you talked to someone? You seem under the weather, too, so you should do something about it. The owner of the store in Gion, the one who placed that special order in three colors, told me something. A nightclub proprietress—the one who wants our bags in different designs—said one of her regulars, a manicurist, told her about an interesting doctor. It might be good for you to see this doctor for a change of pace."

"What's with the whole 'someone knows someone who knows someone'? And when you say 'doctor,' do you mean, like, a mental health professional?"

"Yup. If I remember correctly, the practice is close to our store. It might make you feel better just to have someone listen to your problems."

Tomoka felt she was being accused of being neurotic, which she didn't appreciate. But the reality was that her stomach hurt and three employees had quit. It was Junko who had to find their replacements, and considering the trouble Junko had to go through, Tomoka couldn't disregard her opinions.

"Fine," said Tomoka. "Where do I need to go?"

"So, that's why I'm here."

Tomoka looked up. She had been looking at her feet not because she was nervous about speaking to a psychiatrist but because she was furious.

In the cramped examination room, the doctor, seated only an arm's length away, was swaying back and forth. And he was hiccupping repeatedly.

Hic! "I see." *Hic!* "That's how"—*hic!*—"it is."

The doctor's eyes glistened, and his face beamed with a sloppy grin. *Is this really the reputable mental health clinic?* Tomoka wondered. The doctor was clearly drunk.

"Have you been drinking alcohol, doctor? Are you drunk?"

"No, no, no." The doctor chuckled. "Not alcohol. Tea. Catnip tea. I only had a sip, but man, it's pretty strong. And, who are you again?"

"Tomoka Takamine. Were you listening to anything I said?"

"Yes, of course. Would you like some catnip tea, Ms. Takamine?"

"No, thank you. I try not to consume anything I'm not used to."

"Don't be that way. It's delicious. It'll make you feel warm and fuzzy. Chitose, can you bring us some tea?" the doctor called out toward the curtains.

A moment later, the nurse entered. She placed a teacup on the desk, but it was empty. Tomoka's expression twisted into a scowl. It wasn't that she wanted to drink the tea, but she wondered what was going on.

"Um . . . where's the tea?"

"Oh, I'm sorry. It looked delicious, so I drank it." The nurse let out a high-pitched giggle and disappeared into the back again.

What's up with this clinic? Is this a joke?

The doctor, perhaps regaining a bit of sobriety, smiled. "I beg your pardon . . . Ms. Takamine, was it? So, what was your issue again?"

The doctor had not heard a single word she'd said after all. She hardened her expression, determined to make him do his job since she was there.

"I want to know how I can be more tolerant of other

people's sloppiness. I don't want to be constantly infuriated by careless, indifferent people—for instance, doctors who don't pay attention to their patients. Oh, I'm not referring to you, doctor. What can I do to stop caring about those kinds of people? I know that I should only care that I'm doing things the right way."

"You say strange things," the doctor said, tilting his head. He chuckled somewhat mockingly.

Tomoka felt her irritation flare. "What do you mean?" she snapped.

"Because you're not at all doing things the right way. If anything, you're doing everything in the wrong way." He burst into laughter.

Tomoka's mouth fell open. She'd received negative feedback before, but this was the first time anyone had said she was not doing things the right way. She found it hard to find the words to respond.

"So," continued the doctor, "let's go for an aggressive treatment and prescribe you a strong cat. I'll give you a two-week dose, so make sure you take it regularly. Chitose, please bring the cat," he called out toward the curtains, but there was no reply.

"Chitose?"

"Yes, yes." The nurse came back into the room. She had seemed quite unfriendly at the reception desk earlier, but now she was all smiles. The pet carrier swung gently in her hands. "A cat? Again?" she asked.

"How much catnip tea have you had, Chitose?"

Chitose giggled. "How much? Who knows? There are so many cats. Everywhere. Just ignore them!" She let out another high-pitched laugh, placed the carrier on the desk, and left.

"Good grief. Sorry about that. Since our scheduled patients have showed no signs of ever arriving, we thought we'd have a quick drink . . . Well, and then along came a new patient. Humans, I tell you, get worked up over the silliest things."

"Excuse me?" Tomoka's eyes widened in outrage. "Did you just say 'the silliest things'?"

"No, no. I said no such thing. Oh, boy, no more catnip tea for a while. Just wait here for a moment. I'll get the supplies for you," said the doctor, and he left the room.

Sitting alone, Tomoka, still unable to make heads or tails of what was happening, peered into the pet carrier. She gasped. There really was a cat inside.

It had clear blue eyes like gems. Its delicate coat was white with some dark brown around its ears and eyes.

How elegant. How lovely. The cat's looking right at me.

"Oh, *wow*." The words escaped Tomoka's lips unconsciously. She couldn't help but tremble at the cat's cuteness. It rested its front paws on the door of the carrier.

The paw pads.

Each roundish white paw was adorned with four pink adzuki bean–sized bumps, and in the center was a small Mount Fuji–like mound. Despite its being fluffy all over, the undersides of the cat's paws were fleshy.

The cat stared intently back at Tomoka with its blue eyes while flicking its paw back and forth. *Let me out of here.* That was what it seemed to be pleading. Tomoka reached for the carrier. Just as she was about to open it, the doctor returned.

"What is it? Is something wrong?"

"N-no. I didn't do— I would never touch a cat without permission. I always do the right thing. By the way, what do you want me to do with this cat? Don't tell me you think this will provide me emotional support or something."

"Emotional support? That's ridiculous. Cats don't provide emotional support. They just sit there and do whatever they like. But they do say 'A cat is the root of all illnesses.' Or wait, was it 'the cure for all illnesses'?" The doctor tilted his head.

Whether it was "root" or "cure" made all the difference.

"Oh no, am I still drunk? Anyway, cats can cure most things. In this bag, you'll find supplies and an instruction leaflet—please make sure to read it carefully when you get home. This cat packs a punch right from the get-go, so don't get startled. You'll gradually get used to it. Ms. Takamine, are you listening to me?"

The doctor's question caught Tomoka off guard. Her attention had been absorbed by the cat's blue eyes. "Y-yes, I'm listening, of course. I always listen to people properly. So, I can keep this cat for two weeks?"

"Yes, you may. Now, take care." The doctor smiled brightly.

Clutching the paper bag and pet carrier, Tomoka left the examination room. The nurse was sleeping with her mouth open at the reception window. *How sloppy,* thought Tomoka.

When she looked inside the paper bag, she found a cheap-looking bowl and a package of unbranded kibble. She decided to read the instruction leaflet.

> **NAME:** Tank. Male. Two years old. American shorthair. Feed moderate amounts of cat food in the morning and at night. Water bowl must always be full. Clean kitty litter as needed. Due to his energetic nature, it's important to provide him with a sufficient amount of space indoors, and do remove any hazardous objects from his reach. He needs

> at least thirty minutes of exercise each day. If this is not possible, please equip him with toys so he can play alone. That's all.

Tomoka raised an eyebrow. The cat in the carrier was fluffy. She knew only as much about cats as the average person, but no matter how she looked at it, this cat was not an American shorthair.

"How careless are they?"

Seething with anger, Tomoka glared at the sleeping nurse. *This food, this instruction leaflet—all useless. I'm going to do my own research on how to take care of this cat properly.*

The cat started to scratch at the door of the carrier. Tomoka caught a glimpse of his tiny paw pads.

She let out a sigh and rushed home.

Ten days later, Tomoka, Junko, and Mitsuki, the senior assistant whom Junko had somehow convinced to come back, were meeting about their new collection on the store's second floor. They exchanged thoughts on the many sketches laid out on the table, each showcasing designs that varied in style and price point.

As Tomoka contemplated the sketch of a leather shoulder

bag she had designed, she murmured, “What about a cat print?”

“Cat?”

“Yes, cat.”

“It’s not a bad idea, but won’t it deviate from our theme for this collection—‘everyday accessories for the working woman’?” asked Junko doubtfully.

Indeed. Tomoka looked at the sketches side by side. They were using soft, lightweight leather for the bag, and it was capacious enough to fit A4-sized documents. It could be decorated with feminine charms like fringe or tassels, and besides their store’s classic colors, they were producing the bag in a limited-edition dusty rose. A versatile style suitable for both professional and personal use. If a cute cat print was added to the design, it instantly became more casual and deviated from their theme. She understood that without being told.

“Exactly. It’s supposed to be a capacious bag that’s formal enough to take to a last-minute business meeting. Even in professional settings, women always carry a lot of things in their bags. Plus, it has to fulfill our ideal customer’s desire to be chic.”

“Yeah, that sounds good. So, among these design sketches—”

"What if we incorporate a cat print into the designs?" asked Tomoka.

The seriousness of Tomoka's tone caused Junko to swivel around and look at her. "Oh, boy, you're repeating yourself now. What's the deal? Why are you insisting on the cat print?" she asked.

"Won't adding prints or embossing make the bags less work appropriate? And a cat print especially feels too cutesy," added Mitsuki.

Cats are too cutesy. That's for sure. Tomoka bit her lip.

"You're right. It's too cutesy, way too cutesy . . . but what if we make the print monochrome?"

"It won't work," said Junko and Mitsuki simultaneously.

Tomoka frowned. "You guys don't need to gang up on me. I get it. Let's just stick to our original theme: everyday accessories for the working woman."

She knew they were right. At the very least, she wasn't going to be able to insert cats into this new collection. But her mind tended to wander in that direction, and she'd catch herself drawing cat ears and paw pads with the stylus of her graphics tablet.

And she noticed cats everywhere: TV commercials, the Internet, cat-themed merchandise. She hadn't realized how this world was so full of cats until now. Her cat obsession had even led her to confuse a plastic bag stuck in some bushes outside the office for a white cat just the other day.

Junko seemed to have noticed the recent change in Tomoka. Just yesterday, she'd caught Tomoka going up to the plastic bag with a big grin on her face.

When Mitsuki headed downstairs to assist customers, Junko came up to Tomoka with a worried expression.

"Did you go to the clinic I told you about the other day?"

"I did," replied Tomoka. "It was such a strange clinic. Both the doctor and nurse were drunk. And on top of that, they prescribed me a cat as if it was some kind of a mood stabilizer."

"Drunk? Prescribed a cat?"

"Now that I think about it, maybe it's their strategy to mess with people's minds or, maybe, their lives. But I'm okay. None of it affected me."

Yet, for the past ten days, after closing the store for the day, Tomoka had completed only the essential tasks before heading straight home. And even today, after quickly finishing tidying up, she hurried back home to her apartment.

She opened her front door, tossed away her high heels, and rushed inside.

"Tank, I'm home!"

After a soft meow, Tank, with his beautiful long-haired white coat, approached her with graceful steps. His dark brown tail resembled a fur collar. The moment Tomoka saw the cat, her face softened. Tank had occupied her thoughts all day—Tank lying down, Tank eating his food, Tank stretching to scratch at his toy.

"Come to Mommy," she said, her arms wide-open, but she was interrupted by a sharp reprimand.

"Tomoka, you have to wash your hands first."

Daigo, wearing an apron, peeked out from the kitchen. The delicious aroma of cooking lingered in the air. Tomoka snapped back to reality.

"Oh, Daigo, you're here today, too?"

"I guess. Hey, don't do that. You should wash your hands before touching Tank."

With a huff, Tomoka went to the bathroom to wash her hands. Usually, she didn't need to be reminded to do what was right. It had just slipped her mind today because Tank was so adorable.

"Here, Tank. Come here. Come to Mommy."

Without even changing her clothes, Tomoka rolled onto the carpet. As if moving to a beat, Tank approached with fluid steps. From Tomoka's vantage point closer to the floor, Tank looked even cuter. When she purposely stayed still, Tank sniffed her steadily from head to toe, rubbed his flank against her, and left a trail of fur.

"Show me your paws."

Tomoka held one of Tank's white paws. From above, it looked like a plump clenched fist. When she flipped it over, she found pink paw pads. She gently ran her finger over them, marveled at the peculiar texture. They were soft and elastic like silicone. No, it was more like gummy candy. It felt satisfying to the touch. Tomoka closed her eyes.

"Tomoka, dinner is ready."

She knew she was being summoned, but Tomoka couldn't let go. Tank's paws were too irresistible. Without changing his expression, Tank suddenly withdrew his paw. He turned his backside toward Tomoka and sauntered away.

"Wait, Tank. Let me smell your paw!"

"Stop being silly. Let's eat," snapped Daigo.

Tank was curled up in a makeshift bed of cardboard box and T-shirt. Tomoka took her seat at the table. Daigo had already begun eating.

"Maybe you shouldn't get too attached to the cat. Don't you have to return Tank in a few days?"

"I know. I've been thinking about it," said Tomoka. She was irritated that he'd reminded her of something she was trying not to think about. *He's the one who needs to be more thoughtful.* She frowned.

Daigo and Tomoka had been dating for five years now. It had all begun when they'd exchanged a few words at an eatery where Daigo had worked as a cook, when Tomoka was still a budding designer for hire. Both of them had dreamed of owning their own businesses one day, and a few years later, Tomoka achieved that dream. Daigo, on the other hand, hopped from one restaurant to another, and presently, he was a cook at an izakaya. His days and nights were completely reversed—he always left the house in the evenings and returned after midnight.

To avoid missing each other, they decided to live together. Daigo was conscientious and good at chores and cooking. Things were easy when they were together, so that was enough—or at least that's what she told people.

"Hey, Daigo," she began.

"What's up?" he replied.

"About that conversation we had the other day—what do you think? You know, about going to see my parents. My parents keep asking when we'll come see them. Of course, there's no deep meaning in just meeting them. Just a casual visit."

"Sure," Daigo said lightly between bites.

Tomoka's eyes widened. "Really? When can we go?"

"Anytime. I just quit my job and have plenty of free time."

"I see . . . you have a lot of free time . . ." *He quit. Again.*

She sipped on the miso soup. The broth was rich, and the daikon radish was tender and full of flavor. Daigo, being a chef, consistently whipped up delicious meals. But despite being in his thirties, he was without direction and had a Pollyannaish outlook. Since they'd met, he'd changed jobs more times than she could count. He'd been at the last izakaya for only a short time yet had already quit.

The reality of Daigo's unemployment gradually registered with Tomoka. They had been in their twenties when they met, and Tomoka had been absorbed in pursuing her dream and had perceived his easygoing nature with optimism. But before Tomoka realized it, she'd turned thirty-two. Deep down, she wanted him to start seriously considering their future. If he didn't find a steady job soon, they would never be able to get married.

"I'm sorry," said Daigo, looking up over the rim of his bowl. "I'll start looking for a job right away. But I'm happy to meet your parents while I'm still unemployed if it's fine with you."

"Oh, no, um . . . You must be busy with the job search. We can see them once things are settled."

"I'm sorry."

"It's okay."

When she saw how apologetic he looked, her anger melted away. *I just have to get my act together. I have to do things the right way. Be more dependable.* The thought lifted her sinking spirits.

"So that means you can stay home for a while, then? Lucky you—you'll get to play with Tank more."

"But this guy here mostly sleeps during the day," said Daigo. "Ragdolls are such a calm breed. He looks like a stuffed animal."

Daigo turned around to see Tank, curled up into a ball in the cardboard box, observing them at the table. With Tank sitting in it, the cardboard box looked like a fancy designer armchair.

The instruction leaflet given to them by the doctor was inaccurate. It was clear he was not an American shorthair. He had a long, fluffy coat and blue eyes. There were many similar-looking breeds, but after researching online, Tomoka determined that Tank, with his white and dark brown fur, appeared to be a purebred Ragdoll. And he was more beautiful than the cats in any of the videos. He was calm and never zoomed around or leaped unexpectedly onto high surfaces. About all he ever did was gently tap at his toys with his paws.

“Tank is a quiet cat, huh? That weird leaflet made it seem like he would be mischievous.”

“He really is. A cat as elegant, clever, and beautiful as Tank . . . I wouldn’t mind keeping him,” said Tomoka. She gazed at him dreamily.

The edges of his ears were tinged with a rich brown, while the rest of his coat was a mix of deep chestnut and white. The bridge of his nose was pristine white, while a subtle touch of brown circled his blue eyes. His chubby, whiskered muzzle was white and resembled marshmallows. Yes, he was like a cup of hot cocoa with marshmallows on top. He was so irresistibly sweet, just looking at him made your heart melt.

“Ohhhhh,” Tomoka sighed.

“You’re making weird sounds again,” said Daigo, laughing.

Although he’s currently unemployed, it doesn’t mean he’s a freeloader, thought Tomoka. *As long as one of us is employed, we’ll have enough to get by. There are no problems. Plus, even with a cat around, our home stays clean, and he always looks put-together. Everything is perfect.*

But what did that doctor say? That I’m doing everything wrong? I do everything the right way. I’ve always been this way and always will be.

The next day, a client with an appointment came by the store. She arrived thirty minutes early, catching Tomoka and Junko off guard.

The client owned a clothing and accessories boutique in Gion. She'd taken a liking to Tomoka's bags and had placed large orders in the past. Not wanting to keep her waiting, they ushered her into the office on the second floor. Junko hastily cleared the table, still cluttered with sketches and fabric swatches.

"Oh, just leave things as they are. You seem busy. It's good that your business is doing well." She spoke with an elegant Kyoto dialect, but to accept her words at face value would have been naive. Some Kyoto natives were known to smile as they delivered snide remarks. The implication was clear: being unprepared meant they were careless.

"I'm so sorry, Kozue. Until just a moment ago, I was sketching a design I thought you'd like, and I lost track of time."

"Oh, really?" asked Kozue, picking up a sketch that had been left on the table. "Well, this is quite cute. How unexpected. I didn't know you did these sorts of designs."

She was holding one of Tomoka's absentminded sketches

of Tank. The drawing was simple, capturing his essence without being overly sweet. Ever since she took in Tank, her hand naturally sketched cats. All her doodles were cats.

"Oh, that."

"This is cute. I'm interested in placing an order for a few more of the bags we discussed before, just in different sizes. Is there a way you could cleverly incorporate this cat illustration somehow? Something tasteful, nothing too childish or cheap-looking. Could you do that for me, please?"

"How about a leather charm stamped with foil or a detachable pouch? The main material could be metallic to give it a vintage touch."

"That would be wonderful. There are many cat lovers among the bar owners of Gion—they'll love this. I know someone who adores cats, and she thinks your bags are lovely. Can I bring her with me next time?"

With perfect timing, Junko brought out the sample of the bag. Kozue checked it out and upped her order before she left.

"Now, that was close." Junko let out a chuckle.

"Truly," said Tomoka. "It's all thanks to Tank. But no matter how good of a customer she is, I wish she'd respect our time. Showing up suddenly and saying 'Just leave things as they are,' without caring about our schedule—"

"Um," interjected Mitsuki timidly, "I actually received a call from Kozue asking to move up her appointment."

"Oh no, Mitsuki. Did you forget?"

"I'm so sorry. Ever since the office assistant quit, I've been swamped. I took the call while doing other things, and I just forgot."

She "just" forgot? Tomoka was about to yell at her to get it together when Junko intervened.

"Well, thanks to that, it looks like the design Tomoka was pushing for will actually be produced. Why don't you create a print with your cat illustration? Maybe we can even make it our brand's logo."

"Oh, that's a great idea. And cats are cool right now," said Mitsuki.

Mitsuki was already back to her calm self. She had always had a carefree attitude. When others had complained, she'd been quick to join the bandwagon, yet it hadn't taken much to convince her to return to work. But she was also full of excuses. Life must be a breeze when one was that carefree, but there was no way Tomoka could live like that.

"A print," murmured Tomoka, looking at her cat sketch.

The sketches of Tank all showed his face. If they were serious about using an illustration, this rough sketch drawn for fun wasn't going to cut it. She needed to digitize the sketch to process it properly.

From the moment Tank arrived, he'd been a calm and gentle cat. His movements were leisurely, and he often climbed onto their laps, seeking scratches. He also didn't mind being picked up, and he felt like a plush fur pillow you could pet endlessly. Just thinking about the texture of Tank's fur made Tomoka's expression soften.

When Mitsuki went down to the ground floor, Junko laughed. "You must care a lot," she said.

"Huh? About what?" Tomoka asked.

"The cat. Your face looks, you know, more relaxed. You said you got a cat from that clinic at the corner of Rokkaku and Takoyakushi streets. Seems like you're really fond of it, huh?"

Tomoka's cheeks flushed. Junko had hit the nail on the head. She wasn't aware of her grinning, but it seemed her cat obsession had been quite apparent.

"Yeah, I guess. When you have a cat, you realize they're pretty cute."

"Pretty cute" was an understatement. If Junko saw how lovey-dovey Tomoka was with the cat, she would have been amazed.

"Do you have any pictures?" asked Junko.

"I do." *Naturally.*

She passed her phone to Junko.

Junko chuckled, but her amusement turned to slight astonishment as the deluge of Tank pictures kept flowing. "Wow, that's a lot of pictures. They all look the same."

"What are you talking about? They inspire creativity because they're all so different," replied Tomoka. "Look at this one. The mesmerizing blue eyes."

"Yeah, yeah. It's still surprising. You're a neat freak, so I never thought you'd have a pet."

"Tank is a well-behaved cat. And he's—" She was about to say Daigo took care of him, but Tomoka swallowed her words. Tomoka's main role was to play with Tank, while Daigo took care of everything else. After all, he was currently unemployed.

Junko was aware that Tomoka for a long while had been dating Daigo, who had a tendency to change jobs frequently. She also knew that their relationship had stagnated and that it bothered Tomoka. But Tomoka didn't want Junko to be concerned, so she didn't mention that he had quit his job yet again. She changed the conversation to another topic. As long as she was doing well, she could handle any uncertainties about Daigo's income. So she needed to come up with a hit product.

"Yes, this is it. This is the one."

She looked at her sketch.

The Ragdoll was an elegant cat, one that could be turned into a mascot that was appealing to women. Anyone who felt its blue-gray gaze would sigh with admiration.

And those paws, with their round pads underneath. The first time she'd touched a cat's paw pads, she'd been astonished. They were supple yet springy, with a resilient feel like memory foam. *Is there a way I could use that sensation?* She couldn't think of anything right away. She had to return Tank in two days, but she wasn't ready. She couldn't let him go just yet.

"I'm going to ask for an extension to keep Tank as a model so I can design more prints. I'm heading out, so I'll leave the rest to you, okay?"

With that, Tomoka left the shop.

The nurse at the reception desk looked up as Tomoka pushed open the heavy door.

"Ms. Takamine, you should still have a few doses of the cat left," she said.

The apathetic look on the nurse's face irritated Tomoka. Giving her a closer look, she realized the nurse was a few years younger than she was. She looked composed; perhaps she'd forgotten how disgracefully she'd behaved the last time Tomoka had seen her. Unkind feelings welled up within her.

"Have you had any catnip tea today?" asked Tomoka. "Getting drunk on catnip—it's as if you're a cat."

The nurse glanced up but remained inscrutable. "Was that supposed to be funny? I'll be sure to laugh later; please go ahead into the examination room."

What's with this nurse?

When she went into the examination room, Tomoka was still frowning. Today, it seemed the doctor was sober, too, but unlike the nurse, he had a friendly demeanor.

"Ms. Takamine, you look dreadful! It seems like the cat's not working too well, even though you've been taking it for a while."

The doctor craned his neck and peered into Tomoka's face. She jerked back in surprise, but he leaned in even closer.

"Well, this isn't quite the effect I was expecting. Strange. Maybe the cat didn't agree with you." The doctor scratched his head.

Tomoka was in no mood for this nonsense.

"About Tank, the Ragdoll . . . I was wondering if I could keep him for a bit longer. I've been asked to design some merchandise based on him, so I'd like to observe him up close a little more. I'm the kind of person who aims to do a meticulous job on any project I'm assigned."

"Ragdoll?" The doctor blinked. He turned to his computer and typed something into it. "Oops, my bad. I'm so sorry, Ms. Takamine. I believe I have prescribed you the wrong cat. The Ragdoll you've been taking is a female cat named Tangerine. She works at a cat café, so she should be quite docile." He turned and said to himself, "No wonder the effects seemed mild."

Tomoka rolled her eyes to the ceiling. This clinic was truly bizarre. It was starting to feel like she'd been hoodwinked.

"Um, this is my first time at a psychiatric clinic. Is this what it's usually like?"

"It's a common misunderstanding, but this isn't a psychiatric clinic. We're not a mental health facility or whatever," said the doctor. "Hmm, you've been taking another cat for two weeks." The doctor frowned as he stared at the computer screen.

Tomoka interjected, "Not a mental health facility? I mean, isn't this place called Kokoro Clinic for the Soul?"

"Yeah, we used to go to Dr. Kokoro's clinic all the time," the doctor said. "Both Chitose and I didn't know anywhere else, so we just borrowed the name. It was such a good hospital. Saved our lives, you know. Hey, how about we prescribe you another one on top of the current one? Along with Tangerine, for another two weeks. What do you say?"

Tomoka didn't know how to answer the mysterious doctor, who was not a psychiatrist. *What kind of clinic is this, then?*

"When you say 'another one on top of the current one,' do you mean another cat?"

"You don't have to worry about drug interactions," the doctor reassured her.

"That's not what I'm worried about. It's just that taking care of two cats . . ."

"Is it too much to handle, taking two cats?" the doctor asked.

"No, it's not that," she replied.

"It *is* too much. Of course it is. Would make it impossible to do things right. Let's not go forward with the second cat."

What is he talking about? The doctor's half smile offended Tomoka. Since Tangerine the Ragdoll was so low-maintenance, she was confident she could manage an additional cat. Besides, if she could observe another cat, she might get more inspiration.

"Don't worry. If it's just two weeks, I can care for them both. I'll look after Tangerine and the other cat," insisted Tomoka.

The doctor nodded. "Sounds good. This time, I'll actually prescribe Tank. Oh, and I realize it's a bit late, but let me give you the instruction leaflet for the cat I have already prescribed you."

It was, indeed, too late. Tomoka felt a surge of frustration as she read the leaflet given to her.

> NAME: Tangerine. Female. Four years old. Ragdoll. Feed moderate amounts of cat food in the morning and at night. Water bowl must always be full. Clean kitty litter as needed. She is beautiful, mild-mannered, and likes interacting with people, and thus has a tendency to become clingy. Please maintain a certain distance from her. If you notice any strong side effects, such as hallucinations or delusions, please consult your physician. That's all.

Tomoka felt a twitch in her cheek. It described the cat at home perfectly. She recalled countless times she'd experienced hallucinations and delusions. Maybe another cat would be too much to handle.

"Is everything okay, Ms. Takamine?" Seeming to sense Tomoka's unease, the doctor peered at her intently. "It's too much, isn't it? You won't be able to manage."

"No, no, that's not the case. I'll be fine," she said.

"Oh, good!" The doctor let out a chuckle. "Oh, by the way, if you're going to take the cats in combination, please make sure to finish both completely. If you stop taking them halfway through, you'll build a resistance to them, and they won't be as effective. Chitose, will you bring the cat?"

He should have said that earlier. Before Tomoka could utter a word of complaint, another pet carrier arrived.

According to the Internet, this was apparently known as the night zoomies.

Tomoka was slumped on the floor while the cat darted around her with incredible speed. *How can I make this cat stop?* He was too fast to catch. Besides, cats were not creatures meant to be caught.

Tank's body was like a mochi dumpling. No, more like melted cheese. The American shorthair launched himself from the sofa, bounded off the wall with a swift kick, and leaped onto the table—an acrobatic move she'd seen only in action movies. The force of his landing sent the tablecloth sliding, resulting in Tank tumbling to the floor, wrapped in cloth. Fully entangled, he thrashed about in a frenzy.

Tangerine, too, became agitated, clawing everything in

sight. The two chased each other, toppling everything in their path. Their adorable, cream-puff-like paws had turned into dangerous weapons.

Tank jumped back onto the table, and from there he leaped onto the top of a kitchen cabinet. Tomoka, who had been watching in a daze, suddenly snapped to attention.

"Daigo, catch him. He could get hurt if he falls from such a high place."

"Yeah, you're right."

Daigo, who had been immobilized by shock, reached out toward Tank, who had flattened himself in the small gap between the ceiling and the cabinet. Just as Daigo's hand almost found the cat, Tank twisted his body and jumped from the cabinet like a spring-loaded toy. Daigo and Tomoka held their breath.

Tank landed gracefully, hardly making a sound. It was as if a cotton ball had fallen to the floor. His paw pads, so pink and fleshy and gel-like, absorbed the impact.

"It's no use, Tomoka. Let's just give up and get some sleep." Daigo was nodding off.

Tomoka glared at him. All he'd done was chase Tank around, unable even to touch his tail. She alone had put in real effort to catch him, and as a result, her hands were covered in scratches.

Light gray coat with black stripes, perky ears, and an

oval face. Tank, the American shorthair, was the cat described in the first leaflet she'd been given. He possessed a classical cuteness and a small, determined-looking mouth. His large frame exuded lively vigor.

Tank's eyes were a light, yellowish-brown shade and held a beauty different from Tangerine's blue eyes. Cat eyes were truly mysterious—when you viewed them from the side, half of the sphere appeared transparent. It was like peering through a glass marble.

After bringing Tank home from the clinic, Tomoka had tried to let him out of the carrier in the living room, but he'd immediately hidden in the corner of the carrier and refused to come out. They'd offered him food and water, but he'd remained in his corner, observing them. Unlike Tangerine, who'd warmed up to them on the first day, Tank seemed wary. As night fell and Tank still hadn't emerged, Tomoka and Daigo left the two cats in the living room and turned off the light.

Then, at midnight, the zoomies began.

A curtain was halfway off its rod because Tank had been hanging from it, and there were scratch marks on the china cabinets. Tomoka had had no idea cats could be so wild. Even the usually calm Tangerine was tumbling around. She regretted leaving out the cushions, the mantel clock, and the fancy silverware case.

"Just leave them be. They'll tire themselves out and fall asleep," said Daigo.

"But not before they destroy the house . . ."

"Don't worry—I'll clean up tomorrow. I'll tidy up the living room and give the American shorthair some exercise. He must be stressed, being in an unfamiliar house," Daigo assured her.

"K-tan."

"What?"

"I think the American shorthair's nickname should be K-tan. The Ragdoll, Ta-tan," explained Tomoka.

"Um, okay . . . I'll make sure to play with *K-tan*."

That's right, Daigo's at home day and night now. It dawned on Tomoka that she was the only one who needed to get enough sleep for tomorrow. Thankfully, Tank and Tangerine, seemingly satisfied, fell quiet.

When they awoke in the morning, the living room looked like a tornado had ripped through it. Daigo had promised to clean up, so Tomoka turned a blind eye and headed to the store. Despite her lack of sleep, she thought she could act like everything was normal.

As soon as Mitsuki saw her, she had something to say. "Is all that fur on your back part of the design of your top?"

"Fur?" asked Tomoka. She twisted around to look at her back. Indeed, it was covered in cat fur. She thought she'd given herself a proper once-over in the mirror, but it must have happened when she sat in a chair before leaving the house.

Oh, gosh! As an accessories designer, she usually paid attention to her appearance, yet this was a sorry state of affairs. And it was going to be like this for another two weeks.

"I'm taking care of some cats, and their fur just gets everywhere. My whole house is in chaos because of them."

"Really? But you seem like someone who'd be able to keep cats under control," said Mitsuki. "Oh, by the way, Kozue called yesterday after you left. She asked if you could do her a favor by meeting her cat-loving friend this afternoon."

"What? But that's so sudden."

"I sent you a text yesterday. Did you miss it?" Mitsuki looked up at Tomoka with a touch of reproach.

Tomoka gulped. "Kozue can be so impatient. That's fine. I don't have anything urgent, and it's a weekday, so the shop won't be that busy."

After entrusting Mitsuki with the task of getting back to Kozue, Tomoka worked on some new designs. Time flew by. It was past noon when Kozue's friend came by.

It wasn't just her kimono that was eye-catching. Her bangs were pulled back, and the rest of her hair was gathered loosely. She exuded an alluring charm that made it clear she was a woman from Hanamachi, a district where geikos—as geishas are known in Kyoto—lived and worked.

"I'm Abino from the *okiya* Komano-ya. I'm sorry for dropping by so suddenly, but when I saw Kozue's beautiful handbag, I begged her to introduce me to you."

"I'm glad you liked her bag," said Tomoka. "Komano-ya is a geikos' lodging house in Gion—isn't that right? Are you a hostess?"

Tomoka was overwhelmed by Abino's glamorous aura, but then something clicked. She recognized Abino's face. Because of her graceful, seductive gestures, and wearing entirely different clothes, it took a moment for Tomoka to realize she was the nurse from the peculiar clinic.

"You're a nurse at a clinic in Nakagyō, aren't you?"

"A nurse? Not at all. I'm a geiko in Gion. On days when I'm not officiating at dinner parties with my clients, I wear regular clothes instead of a kimono, but I never dress up like a nurse," she replied with an elegant smile.

The more Tomoka looked at her, the more she saw the similarities. She could only assume that they were really one and the same person.

A side hustle? Juggling being a geiko and being a nurse?

But it was impossible to read Abino's calm smile. If she remembered correctly, the nurse's name was Chitose. Both entertaining and nursing were demanding jobs. Juggling both had to be tough.

"I'm sorry, it's just that there's a nurse named Chitose at the clinic I go to who looks so much like you," said Tomoka. She let out a chuckle.

Abino's expression suddenly changed completely. She looked serious and tense.

"Did you say 'Chitose'? Where did you see her?" Abino pressed her, coming closer.

Tomoka took a step back. "Where? At a clinic down an alley off Rokkaku Street. She's a nurse at a weird practice called Nakagyō Kokoro Clinic for the Soul."

"Dr. Kokoro's practice? Is Chitose at Suda Animal Hospital?"

"Animal hospital?"

The conversation wasn't making any sense. There was a hint of pain in Abino's eyes.

"Huh?"

Tomoka stopped in the middle of the intersection. She looked east and west, then north and south. Somehow, she had walked past the alley without noticing it.

At the corner of Takoyakushi Street, Abino watched her solemnly, looking like a child holding back tears.

"Please wait a moment, Abino. I'm sure it's around here." She circled back down the street, checking each building along the way. But she couldn't find the path that led to the building where Nakagyō Kokoro Clinic for the Soul was located.

"That's funny. There was this dimly lit alley with a building at the end of it. The clinic was on the fifth floor. I've been there twice already. Are we on the wrong street? That can't be."

"So, it's not Suda Animal Hospital you're looking for?" Abino's brow furrowed as suspicion crossed her face. It seemed like their understandings differed, and their conversation was going nowhere.

"Like I said, it's not an animal hospital. It's a mental health . . . Well, apparently, it's not a mental health clinic, but it's a clinic for the soul. It's an odd place."

It was frustrating, and she couldn't explain it. Abino had desperately begged Tomoka to take her to the clinic, yet for some reason they couldn't seem to find it.

Abino looked at her feet, seemingly lost in thought.

Did I dream up that clinic? wondered Tomoka. *No, Tangerine and Tank have wreaked havoc at my house. The cats are real.*

"Is the clinic located in a building called the Nakagyō Building? An old, narrow building with five floors?" asked Abino quizzically.

"I don't know what it's called, but it sounds like the building you described," said Tomoka. "Do you know it?"

"It's the place where Chitose was found. She was born there," Abino said.

This time, Abino led the way as they walked back down the street. They looked up at a building halfway along the block on Fuyacho Street.

Tomoka was dumbfounded. "What's going on? This building should be at the end of a narrow alley."

"This is the Nakagyō Building. It's been here for a long time. If what you said is true, Chitose should be on the fifth floor of this building," said Abino, striding through the entrance.

It was beyond mysterious. This was downright unnerving. She had gotten Tangerine and Tank from that clinic. No matter what, she needed to find out what was going on.

Just as Tomoka remembered, the hallway was dimly lit. As they climbed up the stairs, she glanced sideways at the dodgy-looking tenants, until they reached the fifth floor.

Before Tomoka could explain that the clinic was in the second unit from the end, Abino was already standing at the door. It was obvious she knew this place. Yet, she stood there with her hand on the doorknob, unmoving. She furrowed her brow again and bit her lip. Without a word, Tomoka took Abino's place and tried the door. It was locked.

There was a sudden harsh metallic clang.

A voice startled them. "That unit's empty."

They turned to see a sketchy-looking guy in a flashy shirt walking toward them from the other end of the hallway.

"If you want to see the space, you should give the management company a call. I don't recommend it, though. That unit's jinxed."

"Jinxed?" Tomoka raised an eyebrow. *This guy is odd.* The situation perplexed her even more.

"Yeah. Even though the unit's vacant, sometimes you can hear noises coming from inside. Like people talking or cats meowing. Maybe there's still some lingering energy or something. Anyway, I've warned you. Don't come complaining to me later." He gave them a scrutinizing look as he passed. He specifically eyed Abino before entering the room next door.

"Vacant unit . . ." Tomoka muttered. *This can't be right.*

Abino was already going back down the stairs, so Tomoka walked quickly to catch up with her. When they stepped outside, Tomoka looked up at the building again. It was still facing the street.

"I have no idea what's going on here," said Tomoka. "What is this place exactly? Who is this Chitose?"

"I don't care about anything as long as Chitose comes back."

Abino seemed lost in thought, appearing somewhat stunned and confused.

"Are you okay?"

Abino nodded, but tears welled up in her eyes. "Thank you for coming all the way here with me, Ms. Takamine. I'll be sure to place an order for the bag."

"Please don't worry about that. I'm just worried about you."

"I'm such a mess, you know. I cry at the drop of a hat, whether alone or at dinner with clients. I need to toughen up. Oh, by the way, just behind this building is the real clinic run by Dr. Kokoro Suda—Suda Animal Hospital."

They parted ways, and Tomoka returned to the office, her mind distracted.

"Hey, Tomoka. You've reviewed the website layout for our seasonal products, right?" Junko asked.

Tomoka snapped out of her daze. "Sorry, not yet."

"The developers have been pushing us for an update, saying we won't make the deadline next week otherwise. It's okay to take things easy, but let's not take *too* much time."

Tomoka clenched her fist under her desk. *I haven't been taking it easy. I do things right. I'm a bit out of it because the cats went on a rampage last night. And Abino's sad face keeps flashing through my mind.*

Tomoka had left work early the past few days, but today she worked until midnight to make up for being unfocused. Exhausted, she returned to her apartment to find it shrouded in darkness.

"I'm home. Daigo?" she called.

The living room was silent. Tomoka turned on the light and froze. The room looked exactly like it had that morning—a chaotic mess. As she stood speechless, the front door opened.

"Ah, I'm sorry, Tomoka. I got a last-minute invitation from a friend to go out for a drink." Daigo stomped into the living room, his face flushed. He let out a laugh. "It's a complete mess. Hey, kitty, where are you? K-tan, Ta-tan. Where did you go? Daddy's home."

As Tomoka watched Daigo searching for the cats, she had a realization.

It isn't me who needs to pull myself together.

Nor is it everyone around me who needs to do things the right way.

The one I wish would get his act together is this guy right here.

Even at his age, he still can't hold down a job. It's not clear when he'll marry me. Does he even want to get married? Even if he doesn't, does he truly love me?

"Enough is enough!" shouted Tomoka. Everything she had been holding back erupted at once. "You're too old to just up and quit your job! You haven't met my parents, and you don't seem to want to get married! You have no plans for the future whatsoever! Get your act together! I'm done. I'm done being the put-together, responsible one."

That was right. She had voiced everything she'd wanted to say every time Daigo quit a job and pushed the prospect of their marriage further away. She'd finally arrived at her true feelings. She might act all high and mighty with Junko and Mitsuki, but she had plenty of flaws herself. But she wanted to believe that she had it all under control, that it was okay even if Daigo was aimless.

Daigo's mouth hung open. With a look of remorse, he lowered his head.

"I'm sorry. I didn't realize you were so angry," he said.

Seeing Daigo so crestfallen, she regained some of her composure. Embarrassment began to creep over her.

"I'm not really angry. I just want you to think about the future a little more. You don't have to do anything right away, but just think things through."

Maybe I'm pressuring him to get married after all. But

regardless of Daigo's response, she felt relieved to have expressed her feelings. She burst out laughing.

Daigo also chuckled awkwardly.

"Tomoka, I couldn't say this before because my career has been so uninspiring—"

He was interrupted by the sound of a cat, but it wasn't the usual meow.

"Ta-tan?"

Tangerine emerged from behind a chair. She wasn't her normal self. Her head was down and she was walking strangely.

They heard another noise. It sounded like a coughing fit. It was Tank. He had been running around so much last night, but now he was dragging his paws.

"Hey, K-tan, what's wrong? You seem . . . off." Tomoka got down on her knees and reached out to him.

All of a sudden, Tank threw up; a moment later Tangerine was also vomiting.

"K-tan! Ta-tan!"

The two cats collapsed on their sides. Tomoka's mind went blank. Daigo seemed to have completely sobered up.

"Tomoka, we need to take them to the vet right away."

"The vet? But it's already late. I doubt any veterinary clinic will be open."

"Don't worry, I'll look for one. In the meantime, grab a

towel and wipe up whatever they vomited so we can take it to the vet. They might have eaten something bad."

"G-got it."

Tomoka's hands were trembling. Nevertheless, she managed to follow Daigo's instructions and got both cats into their pet carriers. Then she contacted the vet Daigo had found and they hopped into a taxi. Their destination was a vet in the heart of Kyoto that provided emergency care—Suda Animal Hospital.

Dr. Suda, a man in his sixties with tousled salt-and-pepper hair, wore his white lab coat over his pajamas. His feet remained in slippers as he conducted the examination.

"It looks like they've thrown up everything," Dr. Suda said, as he peered at one cat and then the other.

Under his light touch, the cats settled on the table, and the rest of the examination proceeded smoothly. *Vets are amazing,* thought Tomoka.

Suda Animal Hospital was located on the street behind the Nakagyō Building, where she'd been that day. Because it offered nighttime emergency care, she had expected it to be a large facility, but it turned out to be in a small clinic sandwiched between town houses, with the back of the building serving as a residence. They were led in through the service door instead of the clinic's front entrance. A single light shone in the examination room, which had been opened specifically for this emergency.

Dr. Suda explained his findings from the vomit they had brought in.

"Looks like the cats must have gotten into some houseplants. Thankfully, I didn't have to pump their stomachs, but certain plants like lilies and dracaenas are highly toxic to cats. There are others, too, that you shouldn't have around the house." Dr. Suda spoke calmly with no blame in his voice, and it was as if he were talking not to Tomoka and Daigo but to the cats.

The cats were placed back in their carriers and now looked right as rain.

Houseplants. Tomoka and Daigo looked at each other. There had been one on the living room windowsill before they got Tangerine, but Tomoka had decided to relocate it as a precaution.

"I put it on the highest shelf of the bookcase," said Daigo.

"It must have fallen during yesterday's nighttime zoomies. If only I'd just cleaned it up right away . . . Well, in the first place, the instruction leaflet did say to remove dangerous objects. It's my fault for not following the directions properly."

"No, it's my fault. I said I would clean the house, but I left everything in a mess and went out. I'm sorry, Ta-tan and K-tan. It was Daddy's fault."

"No, no, it was Mommy's fault. I'm sorry, Ta-tan and K-tan."

While the two argued over who was responsible, Dr. Suda brought out the cats' medicine. He remained courteous to them despite the lateness of the hour.

"Thank you so much, Dr. Suda, for seeing us in the middle of the night. You saved us," said Tomoka.

"Animals don't care if it's day or night. And unlike humans, they can't call for an ambulance."

It was true. Tomoka should have researched vets in her neighborhood and where to go outside of business hours. If she was going to take in cats, she should have considered all these things.

Taking a look around the clinic, Tomoka noticed that not only was the building old, but everything inside was as well. The examination tables, the lighting fixtures, the shelves crammed with specimens, and the thick veterinary textbooks were all ancient. Even the microscopes and X-ray machines were showing their age.

Dr. Suda himself was no spring chicken, and the veterinary clinic looked like it had long been rooted in the community. Though it was listed online as offering emergency services, it was probably rare for a clinic this size to see patients late into the night.

"Do you run this clinic alone, Dr. Suda?" asked Tomoka.

"At night, yes. But during the day, I have staff to assist me. If there's anything you're concerned about, feel free to come by anytime. We don't mind phone calls either. Take care." There was a hint of sleepiness in his voice.

Tomoka took the carrier with Tank, and Daigo the carrier with Tangerine.

Daigo took out his phone. "I'll get us a cab."

"Hey, Daigo."

"Yeah?"

"You know, earlier, when you were about to say something—something you couldn't say before because of your career . . . What were you about to say?"

Daigo's eyes widened, a hint of alarm on his face.

"That's, umm . . . well, because my career . . . You know what? I'll tell you once I find a new job. Wait, is that a taxi over there?"

Daigo ran down the street.

Tomoka watched him, exasperation creeping up on her. This was proof that she had to be the one who had her act together. Once Daigo secured a job, she would immediately drag him to meet her parents.

Tomoka climbed the stairs to the fifth floor, her breath ragged. Her legs wobbled under the weight of two cat-filled carriers. After much struggle, she managed to heave open the door to the clinic. She found the nurse sitting at the reception window.

The nurse wore a look of disinterest, but she looked just like Abino. No, upon closer inspection, she appeared more composed than Abino. The nurse looked up.

"Ms. Takamine, you're here to return the cats, right? Please head into the examination room."

Tomoka did as she was told and waited for the doctor in the examination room.

Over the last days with the cats, she found herself pondering, *Maybe I won't find the building again. And if I do, maybe the door will be locked. If it is, Tangerine and Tank will become mine.*

Envisioning life with the two cats, she'd continued to draw more and more cat illustrations. What she'd ended up with was a picture of a cat that was both sweet and sharp. The dark coloring around its ears mimicked Tangerine's features. The evenly spaced stripes on the forehead and cheeks resembled Tank's. She combined the two cats' features and drew eyes that were clear like marbles. She added these illustrations to Kozue's favorite designs, and Tomoka was pleased with the result.

"Things have come together nicely. I wouldn't expect anything less from you! I've been thinking how everything's felt so bland and inflexible recently," said Junko.

"Hey, don't get all high and mighty with me! Just so you know, I haven't suddenly shifted my aesthetics to being all about cute animals. The theme here is a sophisticated sweetness for adults."

"I see. Sophisticated sweetness. That fits the bill for cats. Let's keep our target market the same—working women with disposable income. Women never lose their appreciation for cute things."

As always, Junko figured out the numbers. It was thanks to Junko that Tomoka's passions could come to life. The reliable management of this shop was all thanks to Junko. Without her realizing it, words of gratitude slipped out. "Thank you, Junko."

"Oh, come on—what's gotten into you? You've gone soft. Must be a sign we're growing old." Junko chuckled.

Tank's mischievous nature knew no bounds, turning every night into a full-fledged zoomies fest. But Tank was also incredibly affectionate, constantly competing with Tangerine to show his belly to her. No amount of petting was enough for him, and she joked with Daigo that she was going to get tendonitis at this rate. It was strange that it no longer bothered her as much when her clothes got covered in fur.

Daigo had refused to see the cats off that day. As he was leaving the apartment, he'd looked away from her and asked her to take the cats back when he wasn't around.

The doctor came in, smiling kindly.

"Ah, you seem to be doing well. Looks like the cats were effective," he said.

"Yes." Tomoka nodded. Since she had stepped into the clinic, tears had been streaming down her face. She longed to touch their paw pads one last time. She wanted to glide her finger over the squishy pads to feel that peculiar sensation that couldn't be understood until you actually experienced it.

Cats truly were therapeutic.

"I'm sad to let them go."

"Cats can have that effect. The feeling of not wanting to let go of something warm and fuzzy will stay with you," said Dr. Nikké. "Now, you two did such a great job. I'll be asking you guys for help again soon. Chitose, please take away the cats."

The nurse entered the room. With a cold look on her face, she took the carriers away. Soon there were no cats in the space.

"What's going to happen to them?" asked Tomoka.

"Well, Tangerine will go back to work. You might be surprised to hear that little kitty is a professional through and through. She's popular wherever she goes. The patients are always smitten with her. Tank, on the other hand, lives in a grand mansion with plenty of other cats. He's the youngest, so he's full of energy and mischief. Both cats are cherished," explained the doctor, as if he were discussing humans. Or perhaps the doctor had a perspective that was close to that of the cats.

"All right, my next patient should be arriving soon," said the doctor.

"Dr. Nikké?"

"Yes?"

"What happens when someone comes here and the door doesn't open?"

"The door will open if you want it to open. Now, take care," said the doctor in a gentle yet somewhat detached tone. His smile resembled that of Dr. Kokoro Suda, whom she'd seen not so long ago.

When she left the examination room, the nurse at the reception window said, "Take care," without even raising her head from her work. Once outside, Tomoka looked up at the building. It was indeed the same Nakagyō Building that she and Abino had visited. Yet, something was different.

If she could create more leeway in both her professional and personal lives, she'd like to get a cat. With her life not quite on track, she knew she had to speak with Daigo.

Tomoka looked behind her. There was no more alley, only the tall and narrow Nakagyō Building. She wondered if that room was now locked, but she didn't check.

Mimita

5

Mimita, a Scottish Fold

"Oh, wow, so you're a doctor of animals?" asked Abino as she poured a cup of sake for Dr. Suda, who sat blushing in embarrassment.

Guests at these dinners were usually prosperous individuals like company presidents, lawyers, and consultants. A veterinarian was a first.

"Yes, Abino. Dr. Suda is the most amazing veterinarian," said Ioka.

Ioka was a wealthy man who owned several buildings in Kyoto and was one of Abino's regulars. He was known for his generosity, which made him a bit of a celebrity in the Gion district. With his shiny forehead and flushed face, he looked every bit the big shot company president, but in reality, he was a good-natured gentleman.

"There, keep pouring more sake for Dr. Suda. I owe him a great deal for saving me."

"Really?" replied Abino, pouring the sake with a steady hand.

Dr. Suda, a quiet man in his sixties, perhaps unaccustomed to settings like this, was acting very shy.

"It's an exaggeration to say I saved you, Mr. Ioka. On the contrary, I never expected you to invite me to a dinner in Gion with a geiko—I'm embarrassed."

"What are you saying? You were a tremendous help when I was in a tough spot."

"What happened?" asked Abino.

Ioka scrunched up his face dramatically.

"You know my building in Nakagyō? Well, one of the tenants skipped town. They didn't just take off without paying rent. They left behind a bunch of cats in the unit."

"Oh, *wow*, cats?" Abino glanced at Suda.

He emptied his sake cup and smiled thinly. "The tenant was an illegal breeder," he explained. "They were breeding the cats in the unit and selling them online. But it looked like they couldn't make the business work, so they abandoned the cats and ran away."

"That's terrible. So, what happened to the abandoned cats?" asked Abino.

Ioka, who was tipsy, exclaimed loudly, "Well, we got so

many complaints about the terrible smell, and when I sent the building management company to check it out, it was a disaster. But we did find a few cats still alive, though in critical condition, and Dr. Suda treated them. He and some volunteers helped clean up the place and even held a memorial service for the cats. Just so you know, I paid Dr. Suda for his work and also made a donation to whatever that volunteer organization was called."

"I'm very grateful to Mr. Ioka for his support in that regard. The cat shelter was apparently in dire straits financially."

"But, Dr. Suda, I hear that you treat dogs and cats more or less for free," said Ioka. "You truly are a good person."

Ioka laughed heartily, and Abino joined in. Since patrons paid a premium for a geiko's company, she was forbidden from looking unhappy. But inside, she was heartbroken. When Ioka left his seat for a moment, Abino discreetly asked Suda for more information.

"About that story just now—what happened to the rescued cats? Maybe I can ask some of my clients if they might be interested in adopting one."

Suda shook his head. "Mr. Ioka was generous with his praise, but in reality, we could only save two cats. The rest didn't make it. Both are still at our clinic. When people hear about the circumstances from which the cats were rescued, they're reluctant to adopt them. It was truly a terrible situation, too distressing to describe in this setting."

Suda laughed, but his eyes looked so sad that Abino didn't know how to respond. It was hard to imagine what kind of condition the cats had been in. Afterward, she did her best to liven up the party as always.

After graduating from middle school, Abino left her hometown and started training as a maiko at the *okiya* Komano-ya, eventually debuting as a geiko in Gion. She was turning twenty-six this year.

Once geishas become independent, they have the freedom to choose their own hairstyles, clothing, and living arrangements, but some choose to remain at their *okiya* and work on a salary basis. Abino was one of them. She lived in Komano-ya and worked as a right-hand woman to Shizue, the proprietress.

A few days after that dinner, Abino was walking down Rokkaku Street with her phone in hand. Dressed in casual clothes, she didn't attract the usual stares. Even her hair was down.

"This is the place."

She came to a stop on Tominokoji Street in front of Suda

Animal Hospital. Like the surrounding residences, the hospital building showed its age.

I am really here. With a pounding heart, she was about to walk into the building when she nearly collided with a man coming from the opposite direction who was trying to enter at the same moment. He apologized first.

"Oh, I'm sorry."

He was a plain-looking young man, this side of thirty. When Abino gestured for him to go ahead, he gave a grateful bow and walked through. She followed after him and found that the waiting room looked no different from that of a typical clinic. A poster advertising dog vaccines hung on the wall. The bulletin board was full of photos of dogs and cats.

Abino wondered if they were patients of this hospital. She saw a photo of a cat wearing a pet cone being held by its owner, and a smile spread across her face. The owner was laughing, but the cat looked incredibly unhappy.

The young man bypassed the reception desk and entered the examination room. Abino couldn't tell if he was a regular patient or an employee. Unsure of the protocol, she informed the receptionist of her appointment and sat on the sofa to wait.

A little while later, the young man, accompanied by Dr.

Suda, emerged. When Dr. Suda spotted Abino, he gave a wry smile.

"You really came, Abino."

"You didn't think I was kidding, did you? I'm very serious."

Suda chuckled. "I'm sorry about that." He turned to the young man and said, "Thank you for coming all this way, Kajiwara. I'll be dropping by the center next week."

"Yes. I look forward to it."

The man, his head slightly inclined, was holding a plastic pet carrier. A cat was visible through the mesh panels on the side. The cat was black like midnight. Its nose and mouth were barely visible, but its golden eyes shimmered.

When the young man left, Abino was led into the examination room. Dr. Suda placed a pet carrier on the large stainless steel examination table. It was the same as the one the young man had been carrying just now.

"Was the person from earlier—?" Abino began to ask.

"Yeah, that's right. He took the other cat. Sorry, but the early bird gets the worm, so he got to choose first. But don't worry; Kajiwara will have his hands full with that one. This one's for you, Abino."

Dr. Suda reached one arm into the carrier and effortlessly lifted the cat out.

"A female calico. Probably around two years old. Her

coat is a little scruffy, but it'll fill out nicely soon enough." He placed the cat on the examination table.

The fur around the cat's face had fallen out in places, revealing some scabby patches. She was skinny and noticeably concave from her back to her hind legs. Her predominantly white coat was scattered with black and reddish-brown oval spots, a distinctive coloration that hinted at a spirited nature. Her eyes were a bright copper, and her ears now stood upright.

"As I mentioned on the phone, her kidney function has deteriorated due to the conditions in which she was bred. We're looking at a pet that will require regular vet visits for years to come. No matter how committed you are right now, the amount of care this cat needs might exceed your expectations. I'm sorry to be discouraging, but . . . Abino?"

Abino was not listening. She was in a silent conversation with the cat sitting before her on the examination table.

Nice to meet you, my cat. My calico cat. You look like a fluffy cotton ball. How adorable you are.

"Abino?"

"Oh, yes. I've done my homework about cats. Plus, I had a cat growing up. It was a mixed-breed cat and healthy as can be, but it was quite temperamental and wouldn't allow me to touch her easily. So, I'm guessing this cat . . ."

She assumed this cat would be just as wary and wouldn't

approach her. But then the cat got up and started to rub its nose against her hand.

Abino felt a tight squeeze in her chest. When their beloved cat had passed away, her entire family had mourned it. Since then, her family had avoided getting another cat. Cats had become a distant source of solace, observed only on the Internet.

So why had she suddenly decided to adopt one? And one that came with problems?

"That's how cats are." Suda smiled. "They're shy, but they like to flirt with people. I suppose they have a way of drawing people in. And once you're drawn in, there's nothing you can do. So, Abino, what do you think? You'll need to be prepared to bid good-bye to this one early. Are you still interested in taking the little one home?"

Abino nodded emphatically. The calico cat was no longer just a cat but a living being in the form of a cat—delicate yet with a haughty look in her eyes.

"Dr. Suda, what's her name?" asked Abino.

Suda shook his head. "Just like the earlier cat, she grew up without a name. You can give her one now that she's yours."

"Shall we go to Dr. Kokoro's clinic, my dear?" asked Abino.

Chitose sat atop a traditional Japanese dresser, her butt toward Abino, refusing to budge. No matter how many times Abino called out, she ignored her.

"Seriously, knock it off. Get down already. The taxi's arriving soon."

It didn't matter what tone she used—it had no effect. But she knew Chitose could hear her. The tip of her bent tail was twitching. Her haunches, which a year ago had been so scrawny, were now firm and filled out.

"She's refusing to come to you because you haven't promised her any treats," said Shizue with a laugh. The proprietress of Komano-ya was like a mother to Abino. She dangled a cat treat, and Chitose came down without hesitation. "Look, Chitose. I'll give this to you when you get back."

"Gee, you always lure her with treats," Abino chided.

"Well, if I don't, this one won't ever come near me. It's taking forever for Chitose to warm to me. Well, I suppose that's part of her charm, too."

"I mean, I was fooled myself. When I first met her, she seemed friendly, and I thought, *What a cute cat.* But as soon as I bring her home, she only comes to me when she feels like it. Right, my little Chitose?"

Chitose's gaze remained fixed on the treat in Shizue's hand.

Shizue laughed. "Well, it's your own fault for being fooled. Just like a geisha, it's not about being sweet all the time. Sometimes, you need to be aloof. If Chitose was a geisha, she'd be the most sought-after one in Gion. Oh, look, it's so dark out." Shizue peered out the large glass door that led to the veranda. "Since the downpour last week, the rain gutters on the second floor won't stop rattling. I've got to get a carpenter to look at them. You better get going before it starts to rain. Take care!"

"Thank you, Mother. There, Chitose. Let's go see Dr. Kokoro."

They were visiting Suda Animal Hospital for Chitose's monthly checkup. It had been a whole year since Abino adopted the calico. Abino lived at Komano-ya in Hanamikōji with young maikos and her geisha sisters. Because there were also many people coming and going from the *okiya*, Chitose was allowed to roam only within the inner rooms to prevent her from dashing out. At night, she slept with Abino in her room on the second floor.

In the taxi to Suda Animal Hospital, Abino talked to Chitose through the mesh in her carrier. "Thanks for fooling me, my dear."

Talking to her cat like this had become a part of her everyday life. She spotted the taxi driver glancing briefly at her in the rearview mirror, but she didn't mind.

Chitose no longer appeared as shabby as she'd looked when they first met; her tricolored coat gleamed. Brown fur encircled her right eye, while black surrounded her left. A white blaze stretched from her forehead to her nose, which was pointed and prominent, giving her a haughty appearance.

In reality, she was a cat that rarely responded when you called out to her. She would stare at you intently, as if uncertain what to do, before turning away. The longer she held your gaze, the more disappointing it was when she snubbed you. Just as Shizue had said, if Chitose were a geisha, she would be very popular.

They arrived at Suda Animal Hospital with some time to spare, so Abino perused the photo board on the wall. Most pictures featured cats and dogs, but there were some birds and rabbits, too. With the owners' permission, the photos were taken on the patients' first visit and then again when the animals were fully recovered.

Abino and Chitose's picture was also on the wall, a picture Dr. Suda took of them on the day she adopted Chitose. In the picture, Chitose was still thin and red-eyed, and her fur was unkempt because of a skin condition. As Dr. Suda had warned, Chitose needed frequent medical treatment. In the beginning, they had been at the vet almost every day.

Nowadays, they had to come only once a month for a checkup. Every time Abino saw this photo, she was reminded of the progress they'd made. All that was left was for Chitose to regain her health completely and have her final photo taken. Abino was keen to have a picture of the new and beautiful Chitose on the board.

It was Suda's wife who had begun putting up the pictures. She had assisted Dr. Suda at work, but Abino heard she had passed away a few years ago. This practice was old, both for its building and its facilities, and Suda was the only veterinarian still here. For pet owners seeking the latest and most advanced medical care, this vet wouldn't be ideal.

Yes, I want to do more for Chitose. Abino was gazing absentmindedly at the photos.

"Chitose Takeda? Please head into the examination room."

At the receptionist's prompt, they walked in. Dr. Suda, clad in a white coat, was smiling.

"All right, let's have a look." Suda spoke as if he were addressing a child. Abino always marveled at how effortlessly he examined Chitose, who usually disliked being touched.

After performing the physical examination and blood tests, Dr. Suda said, "The results aren't great."

"I see." Abino nodded. In truth, on her way here, she'd been hopeful that Chitose would make a miraculous recovery. After all, she was still young, so things could improve. But miracles didn't happen. From the day they'd met, Chitose's underlying condition had steadily worsened. "I see," she repeated. Her eyes welled up with tears, but they didn't spill over.

On the steel examination table, Chitose tilted her nose toward Abino, so Abino leaned in, bringing her face down to her cat. Chitose's snout was soft and damp. Abino wished for moments like this to last forever. If it meant advanced treatment was necessary, she would spare nothing.

I'm going to save Chitose.

"Dr. Kokoro, it was you who saved Chitose, and even though she's shy, she's grown fond of you. That's why I'd hoped she could continue her treatment here with you for as long as possible, but . . ."

"Please don't hesitate if you want to get a second opinion. I can provide a referral letter for you."

"I recall you mentioning that you have connections with a renowned animal hospital in the east. You spoke about the advanced research in animal medicine abroad and how this hospital has incorporated those treatment methods. I'll do anything if it means my cat can live even one second longer. Could you please make us a referral?"

"Well . . . to get treatment at this facility will cost more than you think. Not to mention the time it will take. You're a popular geisha, Abino. What will you do about work?"

"I'll figure something out," Abino pleaded.

Dr. Suda let out a bitter sigh. "As I mentioned from the beginning, this cat requires careful consideration. And no matter how ready you think you are, you can never truly anticipate the extent of care animals require. They can't speak up for themselves."

"I understand Chitose better than anyone. Besides me, she has no one else. I'm prepared to go anywhere and do anything for my little one," said Abino.

"I see. If you're so determined, let's consider transferring Chitose to a veterinary hospital that offers advanced treatment."

Abino felt like she could see a glimmer of hope. In the taxi on their way back, she spoke to Chitose.

"Don't worry, my dear. I'll make sure you get better. Let's stick together forever and ever."

Abino closed her eyes. The sound of pattering reverberated around her. When she looked up, she saw large raindrops pelting the taxi's windows, and in an instant, the rain swelled into a torrential downpour.

That night, as always, Abino carried Chitose to the second floor of the *okiya*. She was about to turn off the lights when Chitose approached her. She stared up at Abino, her tail alert. From her expression and gestures, it was clear she was asking for something.

Abino crouched and extended her hand. She was used to being ignored by Chitose when she beckoned her. Nonetheless, she still said, "Come here."

Chitose's black pupils widened inside her copper-colored irises. She sniffed Abino's fingers and nuzzled her face. She rubbed clockwise with the brown patch of fur, counterclockwise with the black, then with her white muzzle. Then she climbed from Abino's hands into her arms. She pressed her front paws against Abino's chest and stood up.

Perhaps it was the environment in which she grew up, or maybe it was her personality, but Chitose was not a cat that calmly allowed herself to be carried. Yet today, she remained serene in Abino's embrace. She licked Abino's cheek with her rough tongue.

"What's gotten into you? You're quite the cuddle bug today, aren't you?"

She lifted her up and gently placed her on her bed. Perhaps Chitose was still feeling a bit anxious from having gone to the vet. Maybe she sensed the impending transfer to another clinic. She wandered around on the bed for a moment before resting her head on the edge of the pillow and curling up into a ball.

Abino lay on the bed, careful not to move the pillow, and gazed up at the ceiling.

"Even if it means we have to go to a hospital far away, I'll do everything I can. Chitose, I know you picked me because you believed I could save you. I can handle anything. I'm not going to give up."

Strangely, Abino didn't feel any anxiety. Taking the first step toward a new treatment option filled her with hope. Chitose would live as long and as happily as any other healthy cat. Lost in the visions of a brighter future, Abino drifted off to sleep.

She was stirred awake by a shift in the air. Moonlight streamed in through the window, casting shadows on the floor. In the darkness, a feline-shaped silhouette emerged. Its ears stood tall and pointed, and the tip of its elongated tail was slightly bent.

"Chitose?"

When Abino attempted to rise, the shadow leaped nimbly through the window. Abino rushed after it and leaned out. It wasn't totally dark outside. Chitose looked up at her from the moonlit cobblestone streets of Gion.

The words on the flyer on the external wall of the animal hospital had been rendered illegible by last week's downpour. Dr. Suda came out while Abino was replacing an old flyer with a new one. He looked up at the sky, then smiled awkwardly.

"How's it going? No luck?"

"No. Whenever I put up new posters, I get some leads, but they always turn out to be dead ends. I check every day with the police lost and found and with the pound, but no luck. Where in the world could she have gone?"

Abino directed the question at the photograph of Chitose printed on the poster. Three months had passed since her cat disappeared.

That night, when Abino had rushed outside, Chitose had still been on the main street. But in the blink of an eye, she'd vanished. In the dark, Abino had desperately searched the neighborhood, crawling on her hands and knees to peer into gutters, getting covered in mud from the bushes, and weeping while she scoured the area until morning. If it hadn't been for Shizue's intervening, she wouldn't have stopped. But now she regretted not having continued for longer. She should've given up everything else and searched harder.

"Seriously, where did she go?" Abino muttered.

"I've told you countless times that pets can get lost, no matter how careful you are. There's no point in blaming yourself any further," said Dr. Suda firmly.

Ever since Chitose had disappeared, Abino had been leaning on Dr. Suda quite a bit. She'd lost the cat that he had entrusted to her. She was sure he must want to chastise her, yet he never once blamed her and instead offered her support. Still, Chitose was missing. The photo on her poster had become blurry and faded in the rain.

"Look, this again. It's not good," said Dr. Suda.

"What?"

Dr. Suda smiled at Abino's vacant expression.

"Don't look like that—like the whole world blames you. This is between you and your cat. You see, in my line of work, I draw a clear line between animals and animals with names. Animals with names have owners, and I consider them a pair. You and Chitose are one such pair. So it's up to you to think and decide what's best for Chitose. It's not something for others to criticize or meddle in."

"I suppose . . ."

Suda's sincere words pierced Abino's heart. Despite the various things people said to her, she held on to one sentiment: regret. After searching tirelessly the night of Chitose's escape, Abino had returned to her room to find the crescent-shaped latch on the window, a common feature in traditional town houses, in the locked position. Yet, the window was open. Abino realized she'd turned the latch without properly pulling the window shut. No matter how she looked at it, it was her fault that Chitose had escaped.

As if sensing her inner turmoil, Dr. Suda said a little sternly, "I'm not asking you to give up. But you have to be reasonable. Look at you. You're going to collapse eventually. And that'll just inconvenience everyone around you."

His words hit a nerve, and Abino felt crestfallen. She folded the tattered poster and let out a heavy sigh. She had no idea how many thousands of flyers she had put up, going even to places outside Kyoto such as Shiga and Osaka. She had done everything she could think of.

Finally, yesterday, Shizue demanded to know how much more Abino was going to do before she was satisfied. At the dinners, Abino's smile had waned, and whenever she had a moment, she was on her phone, gathering information. A professional geiko shouldn't allow tears to smudge her white face powder. And because Abino knew how much Shizue had adored Chitose, she thought it was perhaps time for her to give up.

"Dr. Suda, I was thinking about visiting the building Chitose was rescued from."

"That building? Why?"

"Cats become attached to places, not people. Of course, I don't think Chitose thinks of the place where she was so badly treated as her home. Even so, maybe something meaningful lingers there for Chitose. Laugh at me or call me foolish, but I want to see it for myself."

"There's nothing lingering there. If there's anything, it's resentment." Dr. Suda's brows were knitted. It was rare to see the vet, who was typically so composed, wearing such an expression.

Abino headed to the parallel street. She had already informed Ioka, the owner of the building, of her plans. She'd lied that an acquaintance was interested in viewing the place and arranged to meet with someone from the property management company.

The tall and narrow Nakagyō Building was located directly behind Suda Animal Hospital. Accompanied by the man from the property management company, Abino climbed to the fifth floor. It was the second unit from the end.

The property manager opened the door without hesitation. The room was surprisingly bright; dazzling sunlight streamed in through the large frosted-glass window.

"It's a great deal for this location. The view is amazing. I highly recommend this unit," said the manager, smiling widely.

Abino stood in the center of the room and swept her eyes over the space. The floors and walls were white and spotless. There was not the slightest trace of the sorrowful events that had occurred there a few years ago.

"Are there any openings for mice or cats to get in and out?" asked Abino.

"Mice? There are ventilation pipes, but I don't think mice can get in from the outside. The ceiling and the pipes are pretty secure. It's an old place, so the walls are pretty sturdy, too," replied the manager, tapping the nearest one.

When Abino thought of the many cats that had been trapped within these walls, a chill went down her spine. Feeling queasy, she stepped out of the room. She thought she heard cats meowing, even though she knew it wasn't possible. An unpleasant smell rose to her nose. If Chitose were to come back here, it wouldn't be out of nostalgia. Just as Dr. Suda said, it would be out of resentment.

What Abino found in the unit was closure. After that trip, Abino returned to her cheery self at the dinners. She approached her work with newfound zeal. It was easier to hide her feelings behind white face powder and smiles.

But occasionally, overwhelming regret and sadness would engulf her, leading to bouts of sobbing, even in the presence of the proprietress and her fellow geishas. She was aware that her behavior perplexed those around her, but there was nothing she could do. She continued to visit the building in secret. She had no real expectations, but as far as Abino knew, there was nowhere else for her to try. Leaning against the door of that fifth-floor unit, she called out for Chitose.

"Come back. Come back, my little Chitose."

Abino was on the second floor of Tomoka Takamine's store to pick up the bag she had ordered. It was a bright orange shoulder bag made of genuine leather. It was lightweight and as soft as it looked.

"It's really lovely. Even better than I expected. Thank you."

Abino truly liked the bag, and she hung it over her shoulder in front of the mirror. Tomoka, the designer, was a sophisticated urban woman. And perhaps in deference to Kozue, who had introduced Abino to her, she had taken Abino to her office on the second floor.

She had met Tomoka about two months ago. Their conversation then had been a bit out of sync, and they both felt like they had been caught up in something strange.

"This isn't part of this bag's design, but would you like it?" asked Tomoka. She offered Abino a decorative fob. It was made from the same orange leather and gold-embossed with a cat's face.

Abino's chest tightened.

"It's adorable."

Abino smiled but couldn't stop the tears from welling up. It depicted a long-haired cat, quite unlike Chitose, yet it felt as though her chest were being squeezed. Unable to bear it any longer, she dropped her head.

"I heard from Kozue that your cat went missing. Was the cat's name 'Chitose' by any chance?" asked Tomoka.

"Yes, it was. It's been a year since she went missing. I did everything I could think of, but I never found her." Abino tried to control the wobble in her voice. She knew Tomoka was probably just making small talk. But her tears suddenly spilled out as if a dam had given way. She lifted her gaze, meeting Tomoka's eyes.

"Truth be told, I want to abandon everything, my job and all, and search for Chitose. From the start, Chitose wasn't destined for a long life. I understand in my heart that my hope may be in vain, yet I still want to believe she's alive. I pretend to have forgotten her because I don't want to trouble those around me, but every night, I find myself crying. I'm so, so heartbroken—I don't even know what to do with myself. Chitose was only with me for a year. A year. I seem foolish, don't I?"

By the end of her speech, Abino found herself laughing even as she cried, fully aware of how silly she sounded. She couldn't blame others for making fun of her for being ridiculous and immature.

But Tomoka didn't make fun of her. She shook her head.

"I might have thought that in the past. But I can't stop thinking about the cats I had only for a month. I feel a pang when I see cats online or in TV commercials. Now, *that's* foolish. They weren't even my cats, yet I ended up making cat merchandise." Tomoka looked at the gold-embossed cat on the fob and laughed self-deprecatingly. "The amount of time you spent together probably matters, but less time doesn't mean less love. Whether it's a day or year, human or cat, and even if we may never see them again, there are those who are irreplaceable in our lives."

Abino felt her heart squeezing again. She wanted to thank her, but her lips trembled and she couldn't speak.

Tomoka added, "Why don't you go back there once more? The doctor's very weird, but if you meet with him, just talking to him might spark something in you. Apparently, if you truly want their door to open, it will. So why not give it another visit?"

Tomoka looked serious. Abino knew where "there" was without asking. But she knew things wouldn't be different. She had been back to that old building many times.

"Oh?"

With a start, she realized she'd wandered down the street, lost in a daze. Abino chuckled to herself as she turned from Takoyakushi Street onto Fuyacho Street. Despite knowing it might be fruitless, she decided to visit the place again—for Tomoka's sake, who had shown her such kindness.

Once again, she'd walked past the building. When she turned back, she found herself on Rokkaku Street. The surroundings felt both familiar and unfamiliar. Unsure of where she was, Abino stopped in her tracks.

There was an alleyway between two buildings. It was dark and difficult to see into its depths. But she found herself drawn in.

At the end of the dim and damp alley stood the narrow and tall Nakagyō Building. When she entered, she was met with a vaguely familiar layout and was able to climb the stairs to the fifth floor without getting lost. She'd visited this unit and cried outside its door countless times. Until now, she'd never had the courage to turn the doorknob. It would surely be locked anyway.

Yet, with just a little force, the door swung open easily.

The interior was different from before. It was no longer an empty room. There was no one at the reception window by the entrance.

A nurse appeared, her slippers making a tapping sound against the floor. She was a pale woman, probably in her late twenties.

"It's Ms. Ami Takeda, right? We've been waiting for you."

"Well, yes . . ." Abino was surprised. She hadn't made an appointment, so why had they been waiting for her? Also, how did they know her real name?

"Please take a seat," said the nurse curtly.

What about this nurse? Abino couldn't shake the feeling that she had met her before. *This face. This voice. Who could she be?*

Puzzled, Abino sat down on the sofa. The room was narrow but bright and clean. Tomoka had been right—without her knowing, this place had turned into a clinic.

A male voice rang out from behind the door of the examination room. "Please come in."

Abino went through.

Inside, a man in a white lab coat sat facing her.

"We've been waiting for you, Ms. Takeda. It took you a while, didn't it?"

"You're . . ." Again, Abino couldn't help but stare

blankly. She knew this doctor. "I've met you at Dr. Kokoro's animal hospital a few times. If I remember correctly, you're Nikké's owner."

She'd crossed paths with him in the waiting room of Suda Animal Hospital several times. He was the man who adopted the black cat who had been rescued from this very room just as Chitose had been. She didn't know the man's name, but she knew the cat was named Nikké. Confused, Abino sat on the chair, prompted by the doctor's extended hand.

The doctor smiled kindly. "What brings you in today?" he asked.

"What brings me in?" Abino didn't know how to respond. Apparently, the man before her was a real doctor. The consultation had already begun.

She had no answer to the doctor's question. Nothing was bothering her. Her life was going smoothly, and she was healthy. She herself didn't know why she'd come. Still, she muttered, "My cat won't come home."

"Understood," said the doctor with a smile. "We'll prescribe you a cat." He spun around in his chair, and with his back facing Abino, he called out, "Chitose, can you bring the cat?"

"Chitose?"

The curtains flew open, and the nurse from earlier

walked in. She was holding a pet carrier. The simple plastic carrier was just like the one they had first placed Chitose in at Suda Animal Hospital.

"Chitose? Is it Chitose?"

Doubtfully, Abino grabbed the carrier with both hands. Inside was a round-faced light brown cat.

The doctor asked the befuddled Abino, "Do you live with your family, Ms. Takeda?"

Abino faltered at the unexpected question. "Uh . . . yes. Well, I mean, I'm not sure."

The doctor chuckled. "Which is it?"

"They're not my real family, but I live with people who are like family to me."

"I see. It'll be better if you live with some kind of family. This cat can be quite intense, so his effect might be too strong for one person. Please adjust your dosage accordingly."

"Oh."

"Also, his habits are quite dominating, so the people you live with might feel his impact, but that's neither here nor there. For now, give it a try for ten days. I'll write you a prescription, so please pick it up at reception on your way out. See you in ten days."

"Oh," replied Abino as she gazed at the light brown cat. The cat stared back at her with his round eyes.

When she left the examination room, she sat down on the sofa in the waiting room. The weight of the carrier on her lap felt familiar. Chitose, too, had weighed about the same in the beginning.

"Ms. Takeda?" the nurse called out from the reception window.

Abino handed the prescription form to the nurse, and the nurse gave her a paper bag in return. "There's an instruction leaflet inside, so please make sure to read it carefully. And if you finish taking the cat and you find that your symptoms have improved, you don't have to come back."

"Really?"

"Yes. I'll talk to the doctor on your behalf. I hope you get better soon. Take care."

"But what about this cat?"

"Take care."

"What should I do with this cat?"

"Take care." The nurse's voice was flat, and she did not lift her gaze from the desk.

Once outside the building, Abino read the instruction leaflet, holding the carrier in the other hand.

> **NAME:** Mimita. Male. Five months old. Scottish fold. Feed moderate amounts of cat food in the morning and at night. Water bowl

> must always be full. Clean kitty litter as needed. He is sociable and may appear attached to you, but in reality, he may still be wary. It's important to connect with him to foster a bond, but please be aware that he has a tendency to run if you pursue him. At bedtime, he should sleep in the same room as the patient. That's all.

"What's this? What does it even mean?"

Her mind was filled with uncertainty. She hadn't come into contact with a cat in a year. When she thought of Chitose coming home and smelling a different feline on her, it made her hesitate to even get near one. Yet, suddenly, without warning, a cat had been thrust upon her. Tomoka had said it might spark something in her. *Spark what?* she wondered.

She slipped out of the dark alley and continued walking, but she still felt shrouded in a fog.

Shizue was crawling on the tatami floor, desperately trying to catch Mimita's attention. Beside her, Abino's sister geisha Yuriha was also on the floor, wiggling a feathered toy.

"Mimita, what a good boy you are. Now come over here. Come."

Mimita observed both of them and, on his short legs, approached Yuriha. Then Shizue brandished a cat treat.

"Here, Mimita, come to Mama. I have a treat for you."

"That's not fair!" cried Yuriha. "You're totally cheating, Mother."

Abino watched the two of them fight over Mimita. Shizue was a cat lover, so she accepted Mimita immediately even though Abino had brought him home without consulting her. If anything, she welcomed him with open arms. Yuriha, like Abino, lived at the *okiya* even after she had graduated from being a maiko and debuted as a geiko. In the days when Chitose had been around, these two women had taken great care of her.

Scottish folds had small folded ears, round dumpling-like faces, and short legs. Their adorable appearance made them a popular breed. Mimita had folded ears that stuck to his spherical head. Rather than ears, it looked like Mimita was wearing a headband with a crushed ribbon. His eyes were perfectly circular, and his entire body was round. If it weren't for the light brown stripes and whiskers, he could have been mistaken for a different feline species altogether.

As the instruction leaflet had said, he was accustomed to being around people and would come to you if you called his name. He also liked to show off his charming movements whenever he played. Presently, he was busy swatting a ball of yarn.

"You're so cute, Mimita," said Shizue. Her voice was steeped with emotion. "It's like a hole in my heart has been filled. I'm glad that Abino decided to get a cat again."

"That's true. Abino, you've been so down. I've missed our dearest Chitose, but I'm glad Mimita is here," said Yuriha, her eyes brimming with tears. She burst into laughter.

Mimita was struggling to hold on to the ball of yarn and ended up flipping over.

"Mother, Mimita reminds me of something. Oh, I know. He looks like an *ohagi*," said Yuriha.

"*Ohagi?* You mean rice balls coated in sweet red bean paste or seaweed?"

"Yes, exactly! He looks like a *kinako ohagi*—coated in soybean powder, round, and delicious-looking."

"You're right. If that's the case, I'd like mine with coarse bean paste inside."

"I prefer smooth bean paste. How about you, Abino?"

Yuriha smiled at Abino, but Abino couldn't bring herself to return the smile. They were both completely smitten with Mimita, and it worried her.

"Mother, Yuriha, I've said this many times: I have to return this cat in three days."

The two women exchanged glances and laughed awkwardly.

"Oh, Abino. The fact that you were open to taking in a cat like this shows you're feeling more positive. Can't you ask the doctor at the clinic if you can adopt the cat?"

"That's right. I'll help out with taking care of Mimita as well."

It was as if they had planned this conversation. Abino suspected they had conspired behind her back.

"What are you two talking about?" Abino desperately tried to hide her agitation. She remembered the downcast eyes of the nurse who had told her she didn't need to come back to the clinic. "I'm only taking care of him temporarily, not adopting him. And besides, what you're saying is unfair to Chitose. It's like we've given up on finding her."

"It's not like that, Abino. Even if we adopt a new cat, it doesn't mean we've given up on Chitose. I don't mind waiting for Chitose. And we won't forget her. Still, your happiness matters, too," said Shizue calmly but with a hint of admonishment. She clapped her hands softly and said, "Mimita, come here. Come on . . . No? Here, I have a treat."

She showed Mimita the treat, then scooped him up

when he abandoned his ball of yarn and came bounding over.

"You're a good boy, Mimita. Abino, you haven't held this cat or even played with him once since he arrived. I don't think you've even called him by his name, have you?" asked Shizue.

She pulled up Mimita by the crook of his front legs and held him toward Abino. Because his front legs were short, it looked like he was holding his arms up high in a cheer on either side of his perfectly spherical head.

If things were different, the sight would have made Abino smile. But the more she watched Mimita make adorable gestures, the more her guilt increased. Whenever she thought of doting on Mimita, she felt like she was abandoning Chitose. She felt Chitose was watching her from somewhere.

"Here, hold him." Shizue brought Mimita closer to her.

Abino turned her face away. "I don't want to. Chitose will be sad when she comes back."

Then she hurried to her room on the second floor and sobbed into her pillow.

"My dear, I won't forget you. I won't ever get another cat."

Laughter floated up from downstairs. Mimita was probably happily playing with the two women. He wasn't lonely without her attention.

Still, at night, Shizue brought Mimita to Abino's room. It was impossible to ignore the cat in her small room, but she pretended not to see him. Mimita seemed to restrain his friendly nature and kept his distance. After watching Abino tug the pull cord of an old light, he voluntarily retreated to his woven wicker basket.

Tonight, once again, Mimita sat, attentively observing Abino. There was a hint of longing in his eyes. Was he lonely? Or perhaps he saw through Abino's needs and desires?

As they locked eyes, Abino was reminded of Yuriha's words—"*ohagi* coated in soybean powder." Mimita's round face truly looked like a plump and squishy *ohagi*. Abino loved both coarse and smooth bean paste. They were sweet and filling. She chuckled softly.

Mimita, responding to her faint laugh, leaned back, holding up his short front legs. She was surprised by this gesture. Mimita was looking for a way in. He stepped closer to her and watched. She recalled from the instruction leaflet that if she called out his name, he'd surely come to her. Just imagining scratching that round head of his made her chest tighten. Again, she felt a wave of guilt come over her.

I can't. She turned her face away. It was too convenient to seek solace in another cat just because she was having a hard time. She couldn't accept him like Shizue and Yuriha had. She needed to maintain distance.

After a while, Mimita lowered his front legs. He seemed to have lost interest. His round, soybean powder–colored face looked somewhat lonely.

Abino took Ioka's hand as they walked the short distance to the taxi that had pulled up next to the restaurant.

"Mr. Ioka, the ground is muddy, so watch your step."

"It sure poured down, huh?"

He looked up at the night sky before getting into the taxi. Until a moment ago, it had been raining heavily, but now, there wasn't a cloud in sight. The full moon lit up the wet cobblestones like a giant lightbulb.

"Abino, I'm counting on you for the next one, too. This time, I'm bringing Dr. Suda and the folks from the whatchamacallit volunteer group, so please make sure they have a good time."

"Of course. I'll be waiting."

"The young one in the group—he's going to be surprised to meet a beauty like you. He's an odd guy who only talks about animals."

"Oh, then, we might get along just fine. I'm also odd. I look forward to meeting him."

Abino hopped into a courtesy car with the other geishas. Along the way, her sister geishas got out at their homes, leaving Abino, who lived at the *okiya*, last.

She could see the moon through the car window. It was so beautiful that she suddenly had the desire to take a nighttime stroll. Usually, she wouldn't walk alone at such a late hour, but she thought it might be fine once in a while and got out one street before the *okiya*. With her back to the bustling main street and the car's headlights, she began to stroll, enjoying the lack of people giving her looks in her geisha attire.

When she glanced up, she saw a huge full moon shining a vibrant yellow. It looked like a *kinako ohagi*.

"Oh, my . . ."

Abino came to a halt. As she thought of *ohagi*, the full moon appeared to her as Mimita. A yellow, perfectly round Mimita with ears that looked like ribbons on his head floating in the night sky. It was already strange enough that the moon brought rice balls to mind, but it was more bizarre that she was being reminded of a cat.

"Ugh, I can't stand this."

She turned her face away from the moon.

Tomorrow. Tomorrow, she would give back Mimita and

finally be free from this strange confusion she'd been feeling. She wanted to focus on Chitose, but having Mimita around was distracting her. Yes, she had to think only of Chitose. Chitose had no one else but her. It was too convenient to try to fill the gaping hole in her heart with something else. She couldn't allow herself to be happy when Chitose was still missing.

The moonlight reflected off the wet cobblestones, shimmering brightly. Soon, her whimsical walk came to an end, and she found herself outside her lodging house.

As she reached for the sliding door at the entrance, something startled her. For a moment, she braced herself, thinking that she saw a person's silhouette, but it wasn't. A cat sat at the end of the long shadow cast on the wet cobblestone. Backlit by the moon, it appeared completely black. Its tail stood tall, with a slight bend at the tip.

Well, I never. She squinted to get a closer look. The cat approached, revealing half its body in the darkness. It had a round body and short legs. It seemed like the bent tail was just an illusion.

"Mimita?"

She broke out in a cold sweat. *There's no way.* At this hour, Mimita should already be upstairs in her room. But as the approaching cat came into focus, it became clear that it was indeed Mimita. He had somehow managed to slip out of the house.

How can this be happening again?

Abino extended her hand. Mimita stepped back. Half his body was once again swallowed up by the darkness. His expression looked different, and he seemed cautious. He raised a front leg, ready to run at any moment.

"M-Mimita. You're a good boy. Come here. I'll give you a treat. You like treats, right?"

The more she called out to him, the more Mimita lowered his posture. For an indoor cat, the outdoors was uncharted territory. Excitement and fear prevented him from hearing human voices.

Much less my voice, thought Abino as she bit her lip. For the few days she had taken care of Mimita, even when Mimita had made an effort to approach her, she had pretended not to notice. It was no wonder he didn't fully trust her.

Still, I need to do something.

She knew she had to act right there and then, or else there would be no turning back. But if she took even one step, he would flee. Her body trembled. She was scared. She didn't want to lose a cat again.

"Mimita." Abino kneeled on the cobblestone, not caring

that her kimono would get wet. "Mimita, it's okay. Come here."

She extended her hands slowly. Mimita remained cautious, as if ready to bolt at any moment. Tears welled up in Abino's eyes, and her lips trembled.

"I'm sorry, Mimita. You came to my home, but I've been acting coldly. The truth is, I didn't want to start liking you too much. It felt like if I started liking you, I was forgetting Chitose. I felt bad about Chitose and couldn't properly cherish you. I'm so sorry."

Tears streamed down her face. She had been so wrapped up in guilt that she had been unable to see what was right in front of her.

"Mimita, don't go. Don't leave me." Abino closed her eyes and prayed. *Come back. Come back, my little cat.*

Something cold brushed against her fingertips. Mimita was licking her fingers with his scratchy, sandpaper-like tongue. He nuzzled his round face against her.

"Mimita . . ."

She gently lifted the cat into her arms. He was heavy and warm. As she felt the softness of his long, stretching body, a smile escaped her.

Abino held Mimita tenderly against her body until she was inside the *okiya*. He jumped gracefully down into the foyer as if nothing had happened and, with light steps, padded farther inside. Shizue, who had come to the door, was astonished as Mimita effortlessly slipped between her legs.

"My goodness! Was Mimita outside? He was supposed to be upstairs."

"Could there be a secret exit in my room? It's the second time this has happened."

"Oh no, that would be bad."

They headed upstairs to Abino's room. As soon as they entered, they both froze.

"The window's open!" cried Shizue in dismay. "I double-checked that it was locked before I let Mimita into your room. I must've been mistaken."

Just as it had that night, a breeze flowed through the room. Abino approached the window. It was only slightly ajar, but the gap was big enough for a cat to slip through.

"Mother!"

"I'm sorry, Abino. Because of me, Mimita almost ended up becoming lost like Chitose. I'm so, so sorry."

"Look here. This latch isn't hooked onto the window frame on this side," said Abino, pointing to the crescent-shaped latch hanging from the window. There was a big gap between the two glass panes, and the clasp was not latching onto the bracket. Even though the window was ostensibly locked, it could be opened with the slightest push.

"Oh, my, you're right. When did our window hardware get this worn-out?" Shizue was appalled.

Abino tried opening and closing the window multiple times. How long had it been since the window stopped locking securely? She always checked her windows before leaving, so how had she not noticed?

She leaned out of the window to peer at the exterior walls and roof. That's when she noticed the rain gutters hanging low and pushing against the edge of the window frame. Shizue took a peek out the window.

"Oh, the gutters become dislodged sometimes when it rains heavily. Just wait a second. I'll fix it right away," said Shizue, reaching out to push the rain gutter back into place.

With the external pressure on the window frame gone, the gap between the windowpanes closed up.

"Because of this, the window . . ."

"Hmm? What did you say?"

"No, nothing. This is dangerous, Mother. Let's have a handyman come fix this soon."

"That's true. I'll call them tomorrow."

Abino turned the latch. The clasp clicked into the hasp.

The lock became useless every time the rain gutter was dislodged. It had also rained heavily the evening Chitose had disappeared. Perhaps the window had been in the same unsecured state. There was no way to confirm it now, but it felt like the thorn that was stuck in her heart had been pulled out.

A voice came from outside the room. "Abino, I brought Mimita with me. Can I come in?"

After checking that the window was properly closed, Abino opened the door to find Yuriha standing there with Mimita in her arms.

"Thank you, Yuriha," said Abino. But when she tried to take the cat from Yuriha, Yuriha held on to him tightly with a somber look on her face.

"What's wrong?" asked Abino.

Yuriha shook her head. "I don't want to return him. I don't want to return Mimita. Sis, do you think it'd be so bad if we just adopted him? If you don't like him, I can keep him in my room and take care of him myself."

It was then that Abino realized that it wasn't just her who had been struggling. Shizue and Yuriha also missed Chitose.

They all knew how difficult owning a cat could be. What worked with one cat didn't always work with the next.

Mimita's round face was resting on Yuriha's shoulder. He might seem friendly on the surface, but if they were going to live together, the road ahead was going to be challenging. To earn his trust, everyone in the family would need to make an effort.

Abino planned to go back to the clinic tomorrow. The nurse had said she didn't need to, but that wouldn't do. It wasn't just about Mimita. She wanted to meet with that strange doctor one more time to reassess her feelings.

Abino pushed open the clinic's door, the carrier with Mimita in hand. The nurse sitting at reception looked up.

"Oh, look who's here. How proper of you." The nurse was as unfriendly as ever.

And that face. It was like looking in a mirror. And a voice that sounded just like hers. *That can't be,* thought Abino as she sat down on the sofa.

"Please come in," a male voice called out from the examination room.

When Abino entered, she saw that the doctor was smiling kindly.

"Ah, you're looking good. It seems the cat's done wonders for you," he said.

"Oh?"

Abino sat down on the chair, feeling puzzled. This doctor also looked just like Nikké's owner. Abino would occasionally see him in the waiting room at Suda Animal Hospital, always accompanied by his black cat. Dr. Suda had told her the man worked for some animal rescue organization. Perhaps he was a psychiatrist who volunteered at shelters. The vibes they gave off were different, but their appearances were identical.

Abino decided to ask him a question as a test. "Is Nikké doing well?"

The doctor smiled and nodded. "Yes, I'm very well, thank you. So, did your cat come back?"

"Huh?"

"Did your cat come back?"

The doctor's question caught Abino off guard. The pet carrier on her lap started to jiggle. Even when Mimita was quiet, she could feel the vibrations.

"Yes, he did."

"That's good. Chitose, please take the cat."

The doctor reached over for the carrier, but Abino hurriedly interjected, "I'm sorry for asking this out of the blue, but is Mimita your cat? If so—"

"No, no. He's not my cat." The doctor chuckled. "He's from a pet store. His breed is popular, but apparently, people prefer Scottish folds with flatter ears, and now he's grown too big to be sold. Humans love kittens. They say this one's already past his prime."

Past his prime? Abino frowned, but the doctor looked unfazed.

"The pet shop's a business, after all. They need to do something about the fully grown cats, so they rotate them from store to store. They say that changing up their location sometimes means they catch the attention of new buyers. Let's hope he finds an owner at the next place. Now, shall we?" said the doctor. He swiftly lifted the carrier and stepped toward the curtains.

Abino stopped him. "Wait, please. Where is this pet shop you mentioned? Where can I go to find Mimita?"

"Hmm. I wonder. If you search earnestly, you'll find him, won't you?"

"Please."

The curtains opened, and the nurse walked in. Her brows were knitted into a stern expression.

"Dr. Nikké, instead of making unpleasant remarks like that, why not just tell her?" she said, snatching Mimita's carrier from the doctor's hands. She looked at Abino. "This cat's headed to a shopping mall in Kusatsu in Shiga Prefecture."

"If I go there, can I find Mimita?" asked Abino.

"Yes, but these things are fated. Families flock to the store on the weekends, so it's better if you head there early, I think."

"Y-yes, that's true. I'll go as soon as possible."

"And you don't have to worry about me," said the nurse,

turning her face, which was identical to Abino's, primly to the side. "I just happened to be in that kind of mood on that day, in that moment. It wasn't like I was waiting for you, and I didn't disappear to make things difficult for you. I made the decision and left of my own volition, so I hope you won't keep moping about it forever."

Abino was unable to comprehend what the nurse had just said.

The nurse furrowed her brows again, looking a bit embarrassed, and continued. "There are a ton of cats out there, you know. So quickly forget about me and go pick him up. He seems clumsy and slow, but he's reasonably cute. Don't you think he suits you?"

"Th-thank you—"

Before she could properly express her gratitude, the nurse left the room with the carrier.

What a strange woman. So unfriendly, but apparently, she'd just given Abino some advice.

Despite Shizue's and Yuriha's wishes, Abino had still been hesitant about keeping Mimita. If the conditions hadn't been right, she might have held back. However, the nurse's words settled her feelings.

"Chitose acted like I was being mean or something. I was just trying to be considerate of her," the doctor grumbled.

"Dr. Nikké?"

"Yes?"

"My family and I discussed this. We'd like to keep Mimita if we are fortunate enough to have him. What do you think?"

"What do *I* think?" The doctor laughed curiously and tilted his head. "Are you worried about what I think?"

"Well, no—" she began, and hung her head. She had no idea where she was or who this doctor was. But he was the only person who could give her an answer. Making up her mind, she looked up at him. "What does Chitose think?"

The doctor chuckled again. "That, I don't know. She was putting on a brave face earlier, but cat or not, only the person herself knows how she feels. But to speak from the cat's perspective, it's only humans who become attached. Cats, though small in stature, have their own worlds. From the moment they step into a new world, they're already looking toward the future. No matter how tough that world is. You are unable to release the cat's tail from your grasp not because you feel sorry for the cat but because you miss her. But she can't shake you off, because, even now, she still loves you." The doctor smiled kindly. "It might be time to let go and bid her good-bye."

Bid her good-bye . . .

Dr. Suda had mentioned it on the day she adopted Chitose. Back then, she thought she was prepared. But she hadn't been prepared at all. She was lonely, sad, and desperately holding on. It was only because Chitose had abruptly disappeared that she was able to avoid a painful farewell. Even then, after Chitose disappeared, Abino had clung on.

But now she was going to let go.

Abino closed her eyes. A calico with a bent tail. Shiny fur. The white blaze from her forehead to her snout. Chitose was proud and thoughtful. There was a strong determination in her eyes, and she was graceful even in the way she showed affection. When they were together, Abino hadn't been able to utter any of this, even to herself, but she had so many things she wanted to say to Chitose.

We were together for only a short time, but I was happy. I'm sorry I couldn't protect you. Thank you for coming to me.

I love you. I love you. Thank you.

Good-bye. I love you. I love you.

When she opened her eyes, she saw that the doctor's eyes were closed. She thought he had deliberately remained silent to wait for her to calm down, but a moment later, he began to sway from side to side.

"Doctor?"

"Huh?" The doctor opened his eyes. "Oh, you're done?"

"Y-yes."

"I see. Great. Now you don't have to come back here anymore. Take care."

Abino left the examination room. The waiting room was empty. She recalled the numerous photos plastered on the walls of Suda Animal Hospital's waiting room and the owners sitting alongside their cats on a long bench. While the owners would exchange only brief greetings, the cats in their carriers might have shared a deeper connection. Perhaps Chitose and Nikké had had a conversation of their own.

The nurse was seated at the reception desk. Abino gave a slight nod. As she was about to turn the doorknob, a voice called out from behind her. "You said 'forever and ever.'"

"What?"

When Abino turned around, she saw that the nurse wore a composed expression but kept her gaze downward. "I'm sorry I couldn't be with you forever and ever." She then looked up and smiled thinly. "Take care."

"Oh."

She left the building, confused. When she looked up, she saw the blue sky high above her. As she walked down the alley, she placed a call.

"Hi, Yuriha. Mimita's apparently going to be at a shopping mall in Kusatsu. I thought I'd head there now . . . Do you want to come with me? . . . But what about work? . . . Oh, you're asking Mother? . . . Yes, sure. Let's fetch him together."

She made her way through the narrow alley and emerged onto the main street. The grid of roads had a way of disorienting her. She often managed to get lost, even on familiar routes.

But today she was looking toward the future. So she wasn't going to get lost.

Nikké found himself alone in the narrow examination room. He sat in his chair, gazing up at the ceiling. This was where he was born and raised. Though it looked different now, he could never forget the scent. Back then he had had many companions, but he had eventually ended up all alone. He closed his eyes and quietly let the loneliness pass.

The curtains flew open. Startled, he almost fell off his chair.

Chitose shot him a cool, piercing look.

"What are you doing, Dr. Nikké?" she asked.

"I should be asking you that. Why are you still here, Chitose?"

"If I'm not here, who will handle reception? Who will take care of the cats? Who will look after you?"

"I'll figure something out. Despite my appearance, I'm quite capable, you know."

"Sure, sure, sure." Chitose looked appalled. "If I don't watch you, you'll be napping constantly. Even with your cat prescriptions, you don't put in much thought each time, do you? It's worked out well so far, but what are you going to do if a cat with nowhere else to go isn't welcomed in?"

"Don't worry. I always observe the cats and the people closely before writing my prescriptions."

"Is that true? Aren't you relying on luck and intuition?"

Chitose acted like she could see through everything. Nikké looked down sulkily.

"That's not— Anyway, your patient already came by, so you don't have to worry about me anymore."

"What are you saying? After all this time?" Chitose sighed deeply, looking exasperated. "Whether we like it or not, we're a bonded pair, Dr. Nikké. I'll stick around until your patients come."

"Well, yeah, but . . ." He couldn't stop his lips from curling into a big smile.

There was a noise coming from the entrance. Someone was calling out. Chitose glanced briefly through the gap in the curtains.

"Oh, looks like we have a patient. Hopefully, it's the one with an appointment," she said.

"I don't think so. It sounded like a woman," said the doctor. "Seems like word is spreading about us through the grapevine. I don't even have time to nap anymore."

"What are you saying? You were just napping a moment ago."

"I wasn't napping just now. I was contemplating the feeling of solitude."

"The grapevine might turn out to be helpful. It's what brought my owner here. It may take time, but eventually your patient will come, too. I'm going to see who it is, so pull yourself together."

Chitose retreated behind the curtains, back to her usual aloof self.

After a while, a young woman entered the room looking serious. She, just like all the patients before, had come there based on unreliable information she'd received from someone somewhere. She was jittery and seemed anxious.

After listening to her story, Dr. Nikké smiled as he always did. "Well, then, we'll prescribe you a cat. Chitose, please bring me the cat."